EXE EDUCATION

EXETER MYSTERIES

BOOK 8

SUZY BUSSELL

SNOWSHOES MEDIA

Exe Education
Exeter Mysteries Book 8
By Suzy Bussell

This is a work of fiction. All of the characters, organisations, and events portrayed in this novel are either products of the author's imagination or are used fictitiously.

Ebook ISBN: 978-1-915717-43-6
Paperback ISBN: 978-1-915717-44-3

CHAPTER 1

Angus saw the finish line in front of him and glanced at his smartwatch. Just over fifty minutes. He didn't normally run 10K – half that was his regular distance – but he'd decided to start training for the Exe to Axe in six months' time. To manage a twenty-plus-mile race, a 10K would go some way to kick-starting his running training again.

The finish line was set up near the entrance to Ludwell Valley Park, where the path opened onto a flat stretch of grass. The sun was low now, casting long shadows across the lawn, and the evening light had a soft golden glow that made everything look better. Angus could hear the traffic from the main road, but up here, surrounded by trees and grass, it felt separate from the rest of Exeter city.

The last big race he'd done was the Grizzly, a twenty-mile cross-country slog along beaches, fields, and roads on the East Devon coast, but that was a few years ago now. He was itching to do another. When the running-club email had mentioned the Exe to Axe, a similar route but a different challenge, he knew a race from Exmouth to Axmouth would be just what he needed to increase his fitness.

"Have you never wanted to run the London Marathon?" Charlotte had asked, when he'd told her his plans. Charlotte was his partner in their private investigation business, and lately, his romantic partner too.

"I've thought about it. I could probably get an entry through the running club, but I'm not sure about going up to London."

She'd wrinkled her nose. "I know what you mean. I'd have to come and cheer you on, too, and I hate London. See what I'd put myself through for you."

Angus had smiled. "Maybe one day I'll do it, but for now there's more than enough races in the South West for me."

Angus crossed the finish line and stood for a few minutes to get his breath back, emptying his water bottle in a few gulps. He'd finished the race, organised by the Exeter Runners, in a respectable time of forty-nine minutes. Not quite as fast as he'd hoped, but still not too shabby for a first race. He needed to plan how to fit the extra training in. At the moment, he and Charlotte weren't working on a case, but that might change shortly. They had a stack of potential cases they could take on.

After the run, a few of them headed to The Dolphin, a pub not far from the park. It was the usual post-run spot – nothing fancy, just a traditional local with dark wood panelling, worn carpet, and the faint smell of chips and beer. The bar was busy, filled with the low hum of conversation and the occasional burst of laughter. A couple of fruit machines blinked in the corner, and a football game played on a TV mounted above the bar.

Angus grabbed a Coke and found a table near the window. There were the usual regulars scattered around, plus a man who'd joined the club a few weeks ago. He'd only done the 5K, but he seemed pretty fast. He came and sat opposite Angus and introduced himself as Freddie Barclay. He was well-spoken and dressed in a Tommy Hilfiger shirt and smart jeans he'd changed into after the race. He looked a bit out of place in The Dolphin, but he didn't seem to notice.

After chatting to another club member for a while, Freddie said to Angus, "You don't remember me, do you?"

Angus, who had been about to take a sip of his Coke, stopped short. "Sorry, have we met?" He racked his brain – could Freddie be someone he'd arrested when he was a police officer? He looked for the nearest exit, just in case.

As though reading his mind, Freddie said, "Don't worry, you didn't arrest me. We did meet in the police, though. I was in the force for a couple of years, but I left. It wasn't for me."

"I'm really sorry, I don't remember you."

"That's okay. It was over ten years ago, and I was in uniform. In the background, doing all the monkey work. You were pretty impressive, though. There weren't many detectives that the uniforms liked. You were one of them."

Angus smiled. "So what did you end up doing after you left?"

"I retrained as a teacher."

"Still doing that?"

"Yeah. I'm the headmaster at St Athelstan's."

"I know of it. That's a private school, isn't it?"

Freddie nodded. "It is. Part boarding school, with plenty of day pupils nearby. I live on-site. One of the perks of the job is my own house on the school grounds."

"Doesn't that mean you never really get to switch off?"

Freddie chuckled. "I suppose so, but I love it. The kids are generally much better behaved than in state schools."

Angus had attended a state school in Exeter, and knew of the many private schools in the area. He and his now ex-wife, Rhona, had never earned enough to send their daughter, Grace, to a private school. Not that it mattered: Rhona was a socialist and didn't believe in private education. "Don't you get loads of problems with posh kids telling you their parents will move them to another school, though? A friend who teaches in a private school in Somerset says the kids run rings around the teachers."

Freddie shrugged. "No, not really. When the parents sign up to the school, they know a certain level of discipline is needed. The ethos of the school is to maintain adherence to the rules." He smiled. "So that's my potted history since leaving the police. What's yours? Still in the police?"

Angus leaned back. "I work as a private detective now. Among other things."

"Other things?"

"I have some flats I rent out, but most of the time I'm working on cases."

"Anything interesting?"

Angus thought of all the cases he'd dealt with over the last couple of years with Charlotte. "A few."

"Funny how life changes. Both of us in different careers now. Although, the crowd control has come in handy with the teaching."

"Indeed."

They chatted for a while longer, then Freddie glanced at his watch. "Better head back. Early start tomorrow." He stood, shook Angus's hand. "Good to catch up. See you next week, hopefully."

"You too."

Angus watched him leave, then finished his Coke. He didn't remember Freddie at all, but it had been a pleasant enough conversation. He gathered his things and headed home to his house in Pennsylvania.

The next morning, Angus arrived at Charlotte's house in Topsham and let himself in to find her on a Zoom call with his nephew, Euan. She was sitting behind the desk in her study, gazing at a computer screen.

"Angus is here," Charlotte said to the screen. She stood up, and they kissed briefly, then she gestured to her chair.

Angus sat down. The window showing Euan was half the screen. The other half looked like computer code.

"Hi, Uncle Angus." Euan waved. He appeared to be in some sort of office.

"How's things?" Angus asked.

"Great, thanks. Charlotte's just been taking me through some advanced network security stuff."

Angus glanced at her. She smiled innocently. That meant she was teaching him to hack. "How's your dad?"

"He's fine. Not really seen him. I've been on a training course in Sweden."

Angus raised his eyebrows. "Sweden? Sounds like you've landed on your feet there."

"Totally. I love this job. They're paying me fifty thousand a year already."

"Wow."

Euan looked off-camera and spoke to someone, then turned back. "Sorry, got to go. Emergency meeting with the manager. DDoS attack on one of our clients."

"Er, okay. See you soon."

"Bye."

The screen went blank.

Angus looked at Charlotte, who was standing nearby. "Are you teaching him dodgy hacking techniques?"

"Just passing on my knowledge to the next generation. Neither of my sons are interested in computers, so Euan gets my attention."

"It's so strange that your sons aren't into computers."

"Don't get me wrong, I love them to the moon and back, but I'm bitterly disappointed in their lack of computer interest." Charlotte was serious, so Angus stifled his amusement.

"Let's talk in the kitchen," he said. "I need a coffee."

"How was the run last night?" Charlotte asked, as Angus tackled the barista machine.

"Good. Training for the Exe to Axe has begun. Had a drink afterwards. What did you get up to?"

"Oh, you know … hacked into the Pentagon."

Angus smiled at her joke, but he wouldn't put it past Charlotte to actually hack into the Pentagon.

"I missed you, though. I mean, I know you need to check on your house now and again, but the bed's too big without you."

The kitchen TV was on, switched to the news channel, and something caught Angus's eye. "Can you turn the TV up?"

Charlotte handed him the remote.

"We've been getting reports of a serious incident at St Athelstan's School in Devon," said the newsreader. "A pupil was found seriously hurt early this morning. The boy is in hospital, and is said to be in a life-threatening condition. The school has declined to comment, and police are asking the public not to speculate at this time."

"Wow," Charlotte said. "That's a private school. They're getting rough these days."

"I met the headmaster of that school last night. He's in the running club, came to the pub. We had a chat. He was in the police with me over ten years ago, apparently."

"Apparently?"

"I don't remember him. He was uniform."

"I can't remember most of the people I worked with ten years ago either."

"Sounds as if he needs his police training for the school." Charlotte took out her phone and did a search. "On the school website, it looks amazing. A beautiful old building. But I suppose even beautiful schools hide secrets." She scrolled some more. "Interesting … they're looking for a computer science teacher. I'm not surprised they haven't recruited yet, looking at the salary. You can get triple that working in the computing industry."

Angus leaned against the counter and sipped his coffee. The news report had unsettled him. Freddie had seemed fine last night, but clearly something serious was happening at that school.

"Anyway," Charlotte said, putting her phone down, "have you decided what case we should work on next?"

Angus shook his head. "Not yet. We're back to insurance fraud or following spouses to check for infidelity. It's endless. Good for business, though."

Charlotte wrinkled her nose. "I'm not sure I can face another suspicious spouse. That last one was terrible. Catching him at a naturist retreat with his Pilates instructor was not what I expected."

Angus chuckled. "Yes, that was something else. Who even knew there was naked Pilates?"

"I'm trying to forget." Charlotte opened the fridge and peered inside: a telltale sign that she was hungry but not willing to cook.

"Shall I make us some breakfast?" said Angus.

Charlotte closed the fridge door. "I thought you'd never ask."

Later that afternoon, Angus was drafting an email to an insurance company, stating that he was willing to take on the batch of jobs they'd asked him to do, when his phone rang. The number wasn't in his contacts list. That meant it was a toss-up between a potential client who didn't want to be identified or a call centre trying to sell him something.

He answered, "Angus Darrow."

"Angus? It's Freddie Barclay. We talked last night."

"How are you doing? I saw the news."

"Yeah, I know. It's been a shock. That's why I'm calling. Can we meet?"

"Er, yeah, sure. Do you want me to come to you, or we could meet away from the school?"

"We're in crisis mode here. Police are everywhere, but I can slip away this evening."

"Okay, how about you come to mine? I'll text you the address. Seven p.m.?"

"Yeah, I can do that time."

"See you then."

CHAPTER 2

Freddie was on time, which Angus hadn't really expected. He wasn't sure what the protocol was for a school after a pupil was found so badly hurt, but he imagined it involved a lot of meetings and crisis management.

Freddie came in, his tie askew, dark circles under his eyes. "Thanks for seeing me."

"Can I get you anything?"

"I could murder a cup of tea."

"Come into the kitchen, and tell me how I can help."

Freddie followed him and started to explain while Angus filled the kettle. "I can't stay too long: I've slipped out for a bit and left the deputy head in charge. The pupils are…" He rubbed his face. "Well, it's not a good situation. We're all shocked at what happened, and I need to get a grip on the situation."

"Tell me what happened."

"The boy's name is Oliver; he's in year 11, and he was found in his dormitory before bedtime. It looked as if he'd tried to hang himself, but I'm not so sure."

"Is he all right?"

"Yes. Thankfully, he's in RD&E Hospital in Exeter at the moment, but given time he should make a full recovery. As long as he gets the right mental-health support so that he doesn't try it again. If that's really what happened."

"So how can I help?"

"I'm really worried about the school. This isn't the first incident, although it is the worst. Teachers keep leaving and I can't work out why. It's hard for me to get to the bottom of what's going on. When you're the headmaster, everyone changes when you walk in the room. Not in a bad way, but everyone treats me differently, you know? It's hard to get staff to open up. They think I'll put every little fault into their annual review."

"I'm not sure how I can help," Angus said carefully.

"There's something deeper going on in the school: I'm sure of it. You could go undercover. Come and teach at the school, find out what's going on, and report back to me."

Angus wasn't expecting that. "But I'm not a qualified teacher, and I don't have a subject to teach. I'm not sure how I could do this, unless I go in as maintenance staff."

"You don't have to be a qualified teacher to teach in a private school."

"Really?"

"Yes. It's just state schools that insist on that. Which is their loss. Some of the best teachers are experts in their field, and although their classroom management might not be as strong, often their enthusiasm for the subject rubs off on the pupils, who do remarkably well."

Angus thought about his teachers back in the day. The ones he remembered were encouraging and passionate. Maybe Freddie had a point. "I suppose if they're no good, you just get rid of them?"

"Exactly."

"Well, I never knew that. I just assumed you had to have a teaching certificate to get anywhere near a school."

"So, what do you think? You could come and see what's going on. It would only be for a few weeks."

Angus mulled over taking charge of a bunch of children. *I wouldn't know where to start,* he thought.

Then he recalled that when Grace was younger he'd coached her football team. She'd been eight or nine and not keen on it, but her best friend had joined the team, and where the friend went, Grace followed. Angus had been roped in when it was clear the team would fold without someone to take over.

He'd enjoyed it. He'd got to spend more time with Grace, and it had given him a good excuse to leave work on time. That had been a rare opportunity back then.

"What do you say?" said Freddie.

"I have a partner. A work partner, I mean, and we usually work together."

"Bring him too. Two people looking out for what's going on might get to the truth quicker."

"She's a woman, and I'd need to discuss it with her."

"She could come too. Undercover."

Angus couldn't believe he was actually considering working undercover in a school. Freddie kept his eyes on him, waiting.

"You could teach PE," Freddie said. "No classroom involved. Just get the boys running, or do any sport you like. They all love football, of course. You don't even have to referee – they've all been taught how to do that too."

Angus frowned. Freddie needed help, but an ex-DI wasn't it. He needed qualified teachers, surely?

He was about to say so when the front door opened. The only other person who had a key was Charlotte.

"Hello!" she called from the hallway. "I know I said I was

staying at home, but I missed you and I thought we—" She came into the kitchen and stopped dead when she saw Freddie. "Oh, um, hello."

"This is Freddie Barclay," said Angus. "He's the headmaster of the school where that incident happened."

Charlotte held out her hand and Freddie shook it. "Oh yes, we saw that on the news this morning. I'm Charlotte, Angus's partner. Work and, er, not work..."

"Freddie has asked us to help at the school," Angus said.

"To get to the bottom of what's going on," Freddie added.

Charlotte put her bag on the counter. "I'm not sure a couple of private investigators going into a school would yield much information. Surely everyone would close ranks?"

Freddie glanced at Angus, then back to Charlotte. "I think you should go in undercover, as teachers."

Charlotte blinked twice. She opened her mouth to reply, then closed it. Angus knew her mind was whirring.

"Oh my God, that is amazing." Charlotte's eyes were wide. "I've always wanted to teach in a school! I could teach computer science. You have a vacancy, don't you?"

Angus tried not to gape. She'd never mentioned a dream like that. But there was still a lot they didn't know about each other.

"You're right that we don't currently have a computer science teacher," Freddie said. "The last one left. Not due to what's happening at the school, but to relocate."

Charlotte jumped up and down and clapped her hands. "Fantastic! There's so much I can teach them."

Freddie glanced at Angus.

"Charlotte is an expert in computing and cybersecurity," Angus explained.

Freddie looked surprised. "We've not had a computer science teacher for nearly two years. There's a lack of teachers in the subject. It's even worse for physics. We've managed to keep our maths teachers, but only just."

Charlotte grinned. "I could get the kids hacking Whitehall before you know it." Freddie laughed, but Angus had a feeling Charlotte wasn't joking.

"So what do you say? Will you do it?" Freddie asked.

Charlotte didn't even glance at Angus. "Absolutely!"

Freddie let out a relieved sigh. "It will be such a relief to have someone looking into this. I can't tell you how pleased I am. I can get someone to give you a crash course in classroom management, but to be honest, we have a tight rein on the boys anyway. There's rarely any trouble in the lessons. It's outside the classroom that's the problem."

Charlotte grinned. "That's settled, then. Angus, what would you teach? Or will you take on an admin role?"

An admin role sounded perfect. Why hadn't he thought of that?

"Oh, you could teach PE!" Charlotte was even more excited now.

Freddie nodded. "That's what we were talking about just before you arrived."

"Perfect. This is going to be such fun!" Charlotte suddenly realised what she'd said and grew serious. "I mean, it'll be fun teaching the kids, not finding out the problem in the school. Would we stay in the school, or come home at night?"

"If you're looking into what's happening, you'll need to be there all the time," Freddie said. "Several teachers have apartments in a separate building, away from the boarders, and there's a free apartment in the main building you can have. It's basic, but it has everything. The boarders are looked after by a rota of teachers over the weekends. You'll have to go on that, I'm afraid."

"My favourite book series growing up was *Malory Towers,*" Charlotte enthused.

Freddie smiled. "I'll have to do some paperwork and get a DBS check on you both, but otherwise, you'll be good to go in a few days. I'll be in touch." He glanced at his watch. "I really need to get back."

"Of course. We're already on the DBS register," Angus said.

"Perfect. The sooner you can get into the school, the better." Freddie looked at his watch. "I'd better get going. Thank you so much: I can't tell you how relieved I am."

Angus saw him out, then returned to the kitchen, where Charlotte kissed him on the cheek. "Well, we wanted an interesting case. This will be epic."

Angus shook his head. "I don't know. Going into a school as teachers? We've got zero experience."

"I've taught a few times."

"Not in a school, though. Online, with one person: Euan."

Charlotte stepped back and stared at him. "You don't think we should take the case?"

"We usually discuss it on our own, not in front of the potential client, and make a decision together."

"But you know him already."

"I worked with him a long time ago. I don't even remember him."

Charlotte put her arm around Angus's waist. "Come on, it'll be great! I'm looking forward to getting inside a private school and seeing what it's like. I went to state school and it was rough."

"I didn't say we shouldn't take the case. I just want to have a think about it."

"What's there to think about?"

"This could be dangerous. Something dodgy is going on."

"All the more reason to go. Honestly, if my kids were there, I'd take them out like a shot. We need to help protect the children."

"It's probably one of the children who's doing it."

"You think?" Charlotte pondered. "That would be one disturbed child."

Angus leaned against the counter. He was already in too deep, he could tell. Once Charlotte set her heart on something, there was no talking her out of it.

"All right," he said. "We'll do it."

Charlotte beamed.

CHAPTER 3

Two days later, Charlotte's doorbell rang, and Charlotte looked at the app on her phone. "Great! Sophie's on time."

Angus looked confused. "Sophie?"

"Yes, don't you remember me telling you yesterday? She's an old friend and also a teacher. She's giving us some fast-track training." Charlotte was already heading for the front door. Angus was left staring at empty space.

He heard the two women talking in the hallway. A moment later, Charlotte came back, with Sophie following her. Angus stood up.

"This is Angus," said Charlotte, and stood next to him.

Sophie was in her sixties, with wild, wiry red hair pulled into a ponytail. She wore corduroy trousers and a blouse that didn't match. She seemed completely the opposite of what Angus would have expected from one of Charlotte's friends.

He held out his hand and Sophie shook it firmly.

"Thanks for doing this," Charlotte said. "We're both completely clueless and have no idea what to do in a school."

Angus frowned. "You've told her what we'll be doing?"

"Only the basics. I haven't named the school. And Sophie won't say anything. Will you, sweetie?"

Sophie put her bag down and looked around the room. "Of course not. Happy to sign an NDA, if you're worried." She didn't wait for an answer. "We'd best get to it straight away. There's a lot to cover."

"Cup of tea first?" Charlotte asked.

"Of course. Perhaps we should do this in the dining room? Then we can sit around a table."

Angus caught Charlotte's eye and glanced towards the kitchen. She followed him in. "What's all this?" he murmured.

She pulled mugs from the cupboard. "I told you. She's going to give us the essentials of being a teacher."

"In a few hours?"

Charlotte shrugged.

Angus put his hand over his eyes for a moment and was starting to have doubts about his decision to take this case. "People study for a year to get a teaching certificate, and train at the same time. How are we supposed to learn to be teachers in a few hours?"

"I know, but how hard can it be?" She lowered her voice. "Honestly, I've known a few teachers over the years, and they always act like martyrs, but all they do is look after a bunch of kids. Anyway, I thought we needed some guidance – what's expected, that sort of thing. We need to look as professional as possible."

Angus thought it over. She had a point: they needed to seem as if they knew what they were doing. They could say they'd career-swapped and were training on the job, but the less lying he had to do, the better.

Charlotte dropped a teabag in a mug and filled it with boiling water.

"All right," Angus said. "If it means less lying, I'll do it."

Charlotte came over and kissed him. "I'm rarely wrong, you know."

He slipped his arm around her and kissed her back. "I know."

They went into the dining room. Sophie was laying out pieces of A4 paper on the table. "We'll start with child safeguarding rules," she said, and pushed documents towards them both. "You're ex-police, I hear?"

Angus nodded and they all sat down.

"So you'll be familiar with most safeguarding rules, but it's different in schools. Never be alone with a child in a classroom unless you have no other option. If you are, leave the door open. Is it a mixed or a single-sex school?"

"Boys only," Charlotte said.

Sophie looked at Angus. "That's a bit easier for you. But still, be extra cautious. And as you'll be doing PE, don't go into the changing rooms unless you hear fighting. Even then, make sure you take someone else with you, in case of accusations. If the kids don't like you, they might make up all sorts of things to get rid of you." She paused.

"Right," Angus said. "No changing rooms. No being alone with a child in a classroom."

"Now, this goes without saying: no touching, hugs, or physical contact, unless it's a medical emergency."

Angus glanced at Charlotte. Her eyes were wide, taking in everything Sophie said.

"This also goes without saying. If you suspect a child is being harmed in any way, go to the safeguarding lead. Do you know who that is?"

"I'm not sure," Charlotte said.

"There'll be a poster in the staffroom, I'm sure. But make a note to ask the headmaster, who should provide you with that information anyway."

Charlotte nodded.

"Now, everything you say and do in front of the children must be appropriate. No swearing, obviously, but also watch what you share about your personal life. A teacher in

Bristol got sacked for telling year 10 pupils about her weekend at a music festival. She mentioned taking drugs, thinking that she was being relatable. She was gone within a week."

"Wow," said Charlotte.

"Don't discuss politics or religion unless it's part of the curriculum. A teacher in Manchester got fired for ranting about Brexit in a geography lesson. Another one in Leeds got the sack for showing a year 9 class a TikTok video he thought was funny, but had some very dodgy content in the background. Parents complained."

Angus and Charlotte sat in silence.

"Then there's bullying. Despite endless programmes to stop it, it's still rife in almost every school, whatever the official line is."

"What do you do if you see it?" Charlotte asked.

"You need to reference the school's anti-bullying policy. Read it and make sure you know their internal procedures to tackle it. If in doubt, go to the teacher who's been designated the anti-bullying lead."

Sophie took a deep breath. "Now the really tricky one: classroom management."

Angus was starting to wonder if they'd bitten off more than they could chew. Charlotte in particular: he would be out on the sports field or in the sports hall most of the time, but Charlotte would be in the classroom, teaching on computers. This was the part he was most interested in. How on earth do you manage a gang of teenagers?

"There will most likely be seating plans for each class," Sophie said. "Find out what they are, or the children will sit with their friends and chat in lessons. Make sure you're in the room before them. If possible, give them a task to do as soon as they arrive. A quiz question, or something. It makes them concentrate and stops them mucking about."

"Split up the chatty ones?" Angus asked.

"Every time. Put anyone who looks like trouble close to you. Front and centre."

Charlotte nodded. "What about Angus and PE?"

Sophie took a deep breath. "There are always some kids who are reluctant to do sports. Watch out for stragglers: they may hide in the changing rooms, hoping they won't be missed on the playing field. So make sure you have a register with you and check them off outside."

"Yes, I can relate to that," Charlotte said. "I hated sports at school. I much preferred being in the science lab, blowing things up." She chuckled. Sophie just stared at her.

"I would have thought you'd be in the computer lab," Angus commented.

Charlotte shook her head. "At school, I preferred chemistry. In fact, computers weren't even on my radar then. It was only when I left and went to college that I got into computing."

"When I was at school, we didn't even have computers," Sophie said.

"You must have had some," Charlotte said. "You're not much older than me."

"Old enough to not have computers."

Angus thought he was probably the same age as Sophie. His experience at school was more like hers: there had been no computers at all.

"How long were you a teacher for?" Angus asked.

"Twenty-five years. I started off in a primary school, then realised secondary teaching was what I wanted to do. But when I got there, I found that was a mistake. It's much more stressful dealing with teenagers than younger children: all those hormones. What a nightmare."

"What subject did you teach?"

"Psychology and sociology."

Angus sat up. "I've read a few psychology books recently. *Man's Search for Meaning* really stuck with me."

"Frankl?" Sophie looked surprised. "That's a good one. Heavy, though."

"But powerful. I've also been working my way through *Thinking, Fast and Slow*. Makes me second-guess pretty much every decision I make now." He chuckled.

"Have you read *The Power of Now*?" Sophie asked.

Angus grimaced. "I tried. Bit too wishy-washy for me. But I get why people like it."

Charlotte rolled her eyes. "I've never read any psychology. I just don't get all that mumbo-jumbo."

Angus raised an eyebrow. "You're always saying that most cybercrime is social engineering, which is a type of psychological manipulation. You should try reading some. You'd find it interesting, I'm sure."

Charlotte blinked twice, which Angus knew meant she'd do no such thing.

Sophie pulled out more documents and handed them over. "Back to classroom management. You need to find out what reward system they use."

Charlotte beamed. "Like house points in Harry Potter?"

"Exactly. Most schools will have houses and rewards. Teachers can usually hand out discretionary house points for things like good behaviour, a high standard of work, or even when a low-performing pupil does something that isn't high-performing, but for them is a good job."

Charlotte wrote that on her growing list.

"The main thing is to act like a teacher. I know that sounds basic, but *you* are in charge. You two might be used to handling dodgy criminals and angry exes, but nothing compares to a roomful of teenagers with attitude."

Charlotte raised an eyebrow. "Sounds delightful."

"Tone of voice is your first weapon," Sophie said. "Start firm, not friendly. If you go in all sunshine and banter, they'll eat you alive. Better to soften later than try and claw back control when you've lost it."

Angus nodded slowly, arms folded. "So, calm but assertive?"

"Exactly. Never shout. In fact, drop your voice when they're getting loud. It makes them work harder to hear you, and you look like you've got nothing to prove. That confidence unnerves them."

She stood up and moved to the middle of the room. "Now, body language. Stand tall, shoulders relaxed, hands out of your pockets. Walk the room: don't hover at the front like a target. And make just enough eye contact to let them know you're not bluffing."

She pulled out a few sheets of paper and handed them over.

"And backchat? What do we do if one of them challenges us?" Angus asked.

"Pause, and don't rise to it. Silence makes them uncomfortable. Then say something simple like, 'We'll talk after the lesson. Let's get back to it.' The minute you try to win a battle of wits, you've lost."

Angus smiled. "So, less James Bond, more Buddhist monk."

"More or less," said Sophie. "But don't be a robot either. Use humour if you can, just not at anyone's expense. Show them you care about what you're teaching – and about them, to a degree. Kids respect passion. They can spot indifference a mile off."

Charlotte grinned. "No problem there. I'll have them all hacking the Pentagon before they know it."

Angus shot her a look.

"What about the actual lesson content?" Charlotte continued.

Sophie sat down. "I thought of that, and I've put together a basic plan for you. This is the national curriculum, with full lesson plans." She handed them more documents. "It outlines lessons for each year group for the next six weeks. If you're there longer, I can give you more. Just follow the instructions, and you should be fine. Obviously, it's a bit easier for you, Angus, as a PE teacher. Just get them all out on the field and they can play sports. Computing is trickier. But stick to spreadsheets and programming and you should be fine."

She paused for a moment. "One last thing."

Charlotte and Angus leaned forward intently.

"Parents. Try not to talk to them: they're a nightmare."

Charlotte and Angus glanced at each other. Angus remembered all the encounters he'd had with Grace's teachers, and he guessed Charlotte was thinking about her two boys, Gethin and Rhys.

"Don't get me wrong, the kids are a nightmare, but the parents are a hundred times worse. They want to control everything and think their little darlings can do no wrong. Their little darlings are, in fact, however, the devil incarnate."

Angus chuckled. "So avoid parents if possible."

"Exactly. If they corner you, be polite, vague, and direct them to the headmaster. It's his job to deal with them." She gathered up her papers. "Right, those are the basics. Any questions?"

Charlotte looked at her notes. "I think we're good for now."

"You'll be fine," Sophie said. "Just remember: confident, calm, and in charge. The kids will test you in the first week, but once they know you won't crack, they'll settle down."

"And if they don't?" Angus asked.

Sophie smiled. "Headmaster again. Or threaten to send them to him; that often works."

After Sophie had left, Charlotte and Angus sat in the kitchen with fresh cups of tea. Charlotte flicked through the lesson plans Sophie had given her. "These are actually quite helpful," she said.

"Yes," said Angus. "Though I'm still not convinced we can

pull this off. I wasn't confident before. Now I'm drowning in all the information I just received."

"Of course we can pull it off! We've gone undercover before."

"Not as teachers."

"How different can it be?" Charlotte said. "We observe, we investigate, we blend in. Same as always."

Angus wasn't so sure. But Charlotte was already making notes, her mind clearly racing ahead. Once she was locked on to something, there was no stopping her.

He just hoped they didn't get found out in the first week.

CHAPTER 4

Angus arrived at Charlotte's house in his VW Golf to pick her up. He'd packed the necessities in one large suitcase and found a smaller one for all his PE kit.

He let himself in and was confronted by three large suitcases in the hallway.

He could hear movement upstairs. He went up and found Charlotte in her bedroom, packing yet another case.

She smiled at him. "Hi! Nearly done here. Just a few more things..." She came over and kissed him, then went back to the case.

"Four cases?" He probably shouldn't have said anything, but he wasn't sure why she needed so many clothes. They were only supposed to be going undercover for a few weeks.

She carried on folding tops. "Well, I've no idea what I'm supposed to wear. It's easy for you: you can alternate between a suit and a tracksuit. I'll be teaching in the classroom, so I need lots of different outfits."

"Charlotte, you need to wear boring, sensible clothes. These are teenage boys. They'll hardly see any females, and you are... Well, you may be old enough to be their mother, but it won't stop them thinking things about you."

Her head snapped round and she stared at him. "Seriously?"

"Yes."

She sat on the end of the bed. "Right, so only sensible clothes. I'd better go through the other cases. There are some things I should put back."

Angus shrugged. "Better just sort it out when we get there. We need to get going: Freddie's expecting us at two o'clock." He glanced at his watch. It was already nearly twelve. "Should we eat before we go?"

"Definitely," said Charlotte, with a decisive nod. "Lunch is a great idea."

"All right, then. While you finish up, I'll go and make us sandwiches."

Angus went downstairs and looked around the kitchen. It was probably the finest he'd ever been in. He remembered the first time he'd seen it, when he first met Charlotte. He'd been overwhelmed by the whole house.

There wasn't a day that went by when he didn't appreciate her house in Topsham. Compared with his semi-detached in Pennsylvania, it was chalk and cheese. Charlotte was always asking him to move in permanently, and he did spend most of his time at her place now. But part of him, despite their strong relationship, wanted to keep hold of his house. It wasn't that he was expecting anything to go wrong – but he was in his mid-fifties now and set in his ways. Sometimes it was nice just to go home and have his own space.

He gathered all the ingredients for sandwiches, made them, cut them, and eventually heard movement on the stairs. He went into the hall and saw Charlotte bringing down a case.

"You should have let me do that." He took the case from her as they both reached the bottom step.

"I can carry a case, you know."

"I know, but that looks heavy."

She grinned. "My hero."

"Your hero has also made you lunch. We need to be quick, though."

"Fantastic. If we're eating school food for the next few weeks, we need to fatten ourselves up now! One of those cases is full of snacks and drinks."

They ate in companionable silence for a while before Charlotte pulled out her phone and checked through a list. "I've done everything to prep the house for my absence. Grigore and his girlfriend are staying here while we're away, and Helena will use the kitchen to cook for the women's refuge."

"One thing we haven't sorted out yet is our cover names."

Charlotte thought for a moment. "I used Bridget last time. I might as well use that again. What about you?"

"I've always fancied myself as a Jack. It's a common name, and many authors use it for their heroes these days."

"Jack." Charlotte raised her eyebrows, then nodded. "Okay. Jack and Bridget. What's our surname?"

"*Our* surname?"

"Yes, our surname. We're going to be married, aren't we? That's why we're turning up together. I spoke to Freddie and it's all sorted."

"You spoke to Freddie? When?"

"Yesterday, to check the sleeping arrangements. We'll be in an apartment in the main school building, just like he said."

"Er, what are the chances of a school employing a computer science teacher and a PE teacher at the same time? Won't that look suspicious?"

Charlotte waved her hand dismissively. "Happens all the time. They get couples who can stay at the school. Sophie said lots of people work and live in schools all around the world. They spend most of their working lives doing that."

Angus finished his sandwich, then picked up his glass of water and took a sip. "That sounds like a difficult life. Always at the beck and call of a headmaster. Different rules for different schools. And if you don't like the school you're in, you have to move out and move on."

"Some people like to travel. It's a good way to see the world."

"I suppose so. Okay, so we're sharing an apartment."

"Freddie said they only usually let married couples share, seeing as it's a Catholic school, but as we're there to investigate, he's letting us." She paused. "I have to say, I'll feel much safer with you there at night than I would alone. Apparently, the staff who live-in get tiny rooms. I'd go mad without someone to talk to."

"I take it you're bringing your computing equipment?"

"That's in another case. You didn't think they were all full of clothes, did you?"

Angus looked at his watch. "We should get going. We can pick a surname on the way." He sensed, though, that Charlotte had already picked one.

Angus loaded the cases into the boot of the VW Golf. It took some creative packing to get them all in, with two cases having to go on the back seat.

"We look as if we're emigrating," Angus said, closing the boot with difficulty.

Charlotte climbed into the passenger seat. "I like to be prepared."

As they drove through Topsham and onto the main road, which led to the motorway, Charlotte pulled out her phone. "Right, surnames. We need something believable but memorable."

"Not too memorable," Angus said. "We're supposed to blend in."

"We could just use your real surname, couldn't we?"

"Absolutely not. If anyone checks up on—"

"All right, all right. What about ... what about Harper?"

Angus considered it. "Harper. Jack and Bridget Harper. Yes, that's fine."

"Just fine?"

"It's a surname, Charlotte. It doesn't need to be exciting."

She tapped away at her phone. "Okay, Harper it is. Jack Harper, PE teacher. Bridget Harper, computer science teacher. Married couple, both career changers, here to help out the school. I'll text Freddie now with our names."

"How long have we been married?" Angus asked.

Charlotte looked at him. "I hadn't thought of that. Two years?"

"Let's make it five. Less chance of us acting like newlyweds and blowing our cover."

She grinned. "Five years, then. Still relatively newlyweds, but settled enough not to be all over each other."

"Exactly."

"What about previous relationships and careers?"

Angus glanced at her. "We both used to work in the civil service: we were local council officers in the audit department. That's where we met."

"Bit boring," Charlotte said, looking out of the side window.

"That's the point. We need to blend in, not stand out."

They drove in silence for a few minutes. The Devon countryside rolled past, fields giving way to villages, then going back to fields again.

"Are you nervous?" Charlotte asked, eventually.

Angus glanced at her. "Yes. You?"

"Terrified." She said it lightly, but he could tell she meant it. "I've never taught before, not properly. What if I'm rubbish?"

"You won't be rubbish. You're brilliant at explaining things. Remember when you taught Euan that security stuff?"

"That was one person on a Zoom call. This is a classroom full of teenage boys who probably don't want to be there."

"You'll be fine," Angus said. "And if you're not, we'll figure it out. That's what we always do."

Charlotte smiled. "Jack and Bridget Harper, off to solve a mystery."

CHAPTER 5

Angus turned off a narrow Devon lane and guided his VW Golf through the tall iron gates of St Athelstan's School. Gravel crunched beneath the tyres as the buildings came into view.

"Well, it's grander in real life," he said, eyeing the ivy-draped turrets and tall windows. "The photos don't do it justice."

"There doesn't seem to be any police here now," Charlotte said, leaning forward in the passenger seat and surveying the landscape. "You'd have thought, with a child injured like that, there would at least be a police presence."

"They've probably finished their initial investigation," said Angus. "There's not much more they can do until the boy wakes up and/or speaks up. If he did try to kill himself, there's no reason for them to be there now."

Charlotte peered up at the façade. "It's like a cross between Hogwarts and a National Trust property."

The school was certainly impressive. The main building was honey-coloured sandstone, three storeys tall, with archways, carved stone lintels, and a bell tower rising above the slate roof. Surrounding it were perfectly trimmed lawns, a scattering of mature oaks, and smaller stone buildings that hinted at expansions over the decades. To one side, a narrow, cloistered walkway connected the old structure to a more modern wing, still dressed in matching stone, but clearly newer.

"Wow," Charlotte murmured, pulling out her phone to take a photo. "It's stunning."

Angus parked in the staff spaces in the main car park, a large area with spaces marked out in white paint. Beyond that he could see a cricket pitch, perfectly maintained, with a white pavilion at one end. The peaked roof of a chapel with a cross on the top was just visible through the trees.

"Bet the fees are eye-watering," he said, switching off the engine. "Probably more than my first house cost."

Before Charlotte could reply, the front doors of the main building opened and Freddie Barclay stepped out. He looked more composed than he had during their last meeting, but his eyes were still shadowed with fatigue. He wore a dark suit and tie, the uniform of the headmaster.

"Welcome," he said, striding across the gravel and extending a hand. "Thank you for coming. Let's get you settled in."

Angus shook his hand. "Good to see you, Freddie. This is my wife, Bridget. We're Jack and Bridget Harper."

Charlotte held out her hand and Freddie shook it. "Got it," he said. "Jack and Bridget Harper. Your paperwork will be sorted under those names."

"Lead the way," Charlotte said.

They followed him through high wooden doors into a grand entrance hall. Dark-panelled walls rose to a vaulted ceiling. Portraits of past headmasters watched over the space with stern faces, while the waxy scent of furniture polish and something slightly musty lingered in the air. A sweeping staircase dominated the centre, its bannister polished to a high shine by decades of hands sliding along it.

"Still think this will be fun?" Angus murmured to Charlotte as they walked.

She looked up to the landing above. "Creepy *and* posh. Right up my street."

To the left, through an open doorway, Angus caught a glimpse of what looked like a common room. Boys in navy blazers lounged on sofas: some reading, others talking in low voices. To the right, a corridor stretched away, lined with noticeboards covered in announcements.

Freddie led them past a pair of heavy double doors, down a short corridor, decorated with framed photographs of sports teams, and into his office. The space was large and filled with floor-to-ceiling bookshelves. A heavy oak desk sat in front of a tall window overlooking the sports field. Through the glass, Angus could see more boys moving between buildings, some carrying bags, others kicking a football. A worn leather armchair sat in the corner, piled with papers.

"Take a seat," Freddie said, gesturing towards two chairs in front of the desk. "We'll run through the essentials, and I'll answer whatever questions you have. I'm just glad you're here."

Angus sat down, trying to shake the feeling that he was back at school himself – only this time, he might be the one in trouble. Charlotte sat beside him, crossed her legs, and pulled a small notebook from her bag.

"Has anything changed since we last spoke?" Angus asked.

"No. Oliver's still in hospital, though he's awake now and stable. There's no long-term damage, it seems, but he won't talk to anyone. Not his parents, not the police, not the counsellor we sent. He just stares at the wall." Freddie rubbed his cheeks. "His parents are devastated. They've been here twice demanding answers. I don't have any to give them."

"Can you tell us about the teachers who left?" Charlotte asked.

"Five have gone in the last six months. All were good teachers, all left suddenly. One went to a school in Scotland, another moved abroad, one just quit teaching altogether. When I asked why, they were vague. Personal reasons, time for a change ... those were the sorts of things they said. But I could tell they were spooked."

Angus leaned forward. "Spooked how?"

"Nervous, jumpy. As if they were looking over their shoulders." Freddie frowned as he remembered. "One of them, Sarah Pemberton, who taught art – she came to me a week before she left. She said she thought something was going on with some of the boys. When I asked what, she clammed up. She said she didn't want to make accusations without proof, and she didn't have any. The next week, she handed in her notice."

"Do you have contact details for her?" Charlotte asked, writing in her notebook.

"I will have. Same for the others."

"That would help," Angus said. "We'll talk to them."

Freddie nodded and wrote a note on his pad. Then he got up. "Let me show you round, then we'll get you settled into your accommodation."

Freddie led them out of his office and into the main hallway. The sound of their footsteps on the polished wooden floors echoed around them, rising to the high ceiling. A group of younger boys in navy blazers passed them, their glances flicking curiously towards Charlotte.

"Don't worry," Freddie said, under his breath. "They're always nosy about new staff. You'll be old news by next week."

The tour took them through the heart of the school. Long corridors stretched in every direction, lined with boards covered in notices, house-point charts and formal photographs of sports teams and debating champions. The boys in the photos all looked far too serious to be teenagers.

They passed classrooms with glass-panelled doors. Through them, Angus could see lessons in full swing: boys in ties hunched over chemistry equipment, Bunsen burners flickering, or watching a screen with forced interest. In one room, a teacher wrote on a whiteboard while a sea of laptops glowed in front of the pupils.

"Pupils are grouped by house," Freddie explained, as they walked. "We've got four: Drake, Raleigh, Bodley, and Coleridge, all named after famous Devonians. Each house has its own housemaster and competes to win the house cup at the end of the year. Some housemasters are stricter than others."

"Which house are we assigned to?" Charlotte asked.

"You'll both be tutors for Coleridge House. Mr Brooke is the housemaster and also head of English. I'll introduce you at the staff meeting tonight."

They passed through the library, a grand room with tall windows and row upon row of dark wooden shelves. Books stretched from floor to ceiling, accessed by rolling ladders. A few boys sat at tables, studying in silence.

At the far end, Charlotte paused to take in the IT corner. Half a dozen computers sat on desks, their monitors chunky and outdated. Several of the machines looked as if they hadn't been turned on for at least ten years.

"Don't worry," said Freddie, seeing her expression. "The IT suite is in better shape. We upgraded that a few years ago. These are just for quick internet access and printing."

He opened a side door that led to a small courtyard. They stepped into bright autumn sunshine.

Beyond the library was a long stone building with arched windows and a slate roof. It looked as if it might once have been stables.

"This is where some of the staff live," Freddie said,

unlocking a heavy wooden door. "We've converted the old stables into flats. Most staff don't live on-site, but we keep accommodation available for those who want to live here. Or in your case, need to live here."

Inside, the building was cool and quiet. A narrow corridor stretched ahead, painted in neutral cream, with brown carpet running its length. The doors on either side had brass numbers.

"You're in number 4, which is larger than most," Freddie said, stopping at a door and handing Angus two sets of keys.

Angus unlocked and opened it, then stepped in. The flat was clean but basic. Cream walls, the same brown carpet, and a faint smell of disinfectant. The main room served as both living space and bedroom, with a double bed against one wall, a sofa under the window and a desk in the corner. A doorway led to a compact kitchen with a sink, kettle, mini-fridge, and microwave. Another door revealed a bathroom with a shower cubicle, toilet, and basin.

"It's not exactly five-star," Freddie said, standing in the doorway, "but it's functional. Most staff who live in are only here during the week and go home at weekends."

"It'll do," Angus said. "We're not here for the luxury."

Freddie looked relieved. "Good. Right then, why don't you both get unpacked and settled? Dinner is in the refectory at six, with the boys. Just come along: the catering staff are expecting you. I'll get your staff ID lanyards sorted and give them to you next time I see you."

"Sounds good," Charlotte said.

Freddie glanced around, then lowered his voice. "Look, I know this is awkward. You're here to investigate, but you need to blend in. The staff won't know who you really are. As far as they're concerned, you're just new teachers. Only Miss James, the deputy head, knows the truth. She's discreet, and you can trust her."

"Understood," Angus said.

"One more thing," said Freddie, in the same low tone. "Be careful. I don't know what's going on here, but whatever it is, it's made good people leave and put a boy in hospital. Don't take any unnecessary risks." And with that, he left.

CHAPTER 6

"You'd think that in a prestigious private school they'd have decent accommodation for the staff, wouldn't you?" said Charlotte, looking around the flat.

"Can you cope with roughing it for a bit?" Angus eyed Charlotte warily.

"Of course! It's not forever, and you're with me."

"Well, I know how you like your luxuries."

"I'll be fine. I wasn't always rich, remember. We ought to bring in the cases and unpack."

"I'll get them. Some are heavy, and I could do with a spot of weight training. Build up my stamina for the long run." Angus left the flat.

Charlotte stood at the window, looking out over the fields. Two football pitches stretched in front of her, with a rugby pitch visible in the far distance. She turned and surveyed the flat again. At least they wouldn't be spending too much time here: it was seriously depressing. No wonder they had problems keeping staff.

When Angus arrived with the first batch of cases, Charlotte started unpacking her computer equipment. The small desk in the corner would do for her laptop. Then she moved on to the clothes.

She picked up a pile of tops, turned, and realised the wardrobe was very narrow. When she opened it, there were only four hangers. Why hadn't she thought to bring more? She'd have to live out of a suitcase, and she hated that. More importantly, how would Angus manage? He was a stickler for looking neat and tidy, and although he had fewer clothes than her, he'd struggle with the lack of hangers.

When he arrived with the last of their luggage, she pointed to the wardrobe. "I'm afraid we have a problem," she said.

"A problem?"

"It's tiny, and we have to share it."

Angus smiled. "Freddie warned me beforehand, so I bought a couple of pop-up clothes rails from IKEA. Looking at how tiny this room is, though, I think we'll have to put them in the lounge."

"Very impressive. Why didn't I think of that?"

"Best keep your brain power for the techie things." Angus put his arms around Charlotte and kissed her on the neck.

Angus eyed the fourth suitcase, the one Charlotte had said was full of snacks and drinks. "Shall I put this in the kitchen?"

"Just leave it by the sofa. I'll sort it out later."

Angus was already unzipping it. He stopped. Stared. Then straightened up slowly.

"Charlotte."

"Mm?"

"This is not a suitcase of snacks."

"It is. There are snacks in there."

"There are Fortnum and Mason lemon shortbread in here. And

Magnifici Florentine Selection." He rummaged further. "Is that a Nespresso machine?"

"It's the travel one. It's tiny."

"It's a two-hundred-pound coffee machine, Charlotte. We have a kettle."

"Have you tasted instant coffee? I'm not doing that for weeks. I'd rather drink the water from the football pitch."

Angus held up a box of salted caramel truffles. "We're supposed to be impoverished teachers. Teachers don't eat salted caramel truffles."

"The good ones do."

"If any of the staff see this lot, they'll think we're running a black-market deli."

Charlotte took the truffles from him and put them on the kitchenette counter. "No one is going to see them. The door will be locked, and the biscuits stay in the case. It's not as if we're going to eat them in the staffroom."

Angus shook his head but didn't argue further. He knew when he was beaten. He also knew that by tomorrow morning, the Fortnum and Mason biscuits would be open.

They entered the refectory at two minutes to six. The room was buzzing with noise, and pupils and staff were everywhere. Pupils were queuing in front of the serving counters, where catering staff dished out food. The refectory tables were set out in long lines, and several pupils who had already got their food were sitting at them, eating. Some of the staff were seated, too, at their own group at the far end. Freddie was on the other side of the room, reprimanding a small boy who looked about twelve.

"Do we have to queue up?" Charlotte whispered to Angus.

"I don't think so. Look, a member of staff has just cut in at the front of the line."

"Makes sense. Let's just do that."

They made their way forward, and the woman behind the counter smiled. "Hello. You must be Mr and Mrs Harper."

"That's right. We arrived this afternoon."

"What would you like? There's fish and chips or mushroom stroganoff. If you don't want either of those, we have jacket potatoes."

"Er, fish and chips, please," Angus said, and she piled up his plate with a generous helping. Charlotte had the same, and they made their way to the table where the other teachers were sitting. They were all in deep conversation, but a couple smiled and nodded. Charlotte recognised a few from their earlier tour.

She glanced up. Freddie was talking to one of the catering staff. She couldn't hear what he was saying, though, as the noise in the room seemed to be getting louder and louder. In fact, the noise and the number of people were starting to stress her out. She wished she'd worn her earplugs.

When Angus said something to her across the table, she couldn't even hear him. She took out her phone and sent him a text: *Can't hear you. Too noisy.*

Then Freddie banged a spoon on the table and everyone hushed instantly.

"Thank you, everyone," he said. "Try to keep the noise down, please. I'm very pleased to welcome Mr and Mrs Harper to the school. Mr Harper will be teaching PE, and Mrs Harper will teach computing and ICT."

Lots of heads turned towards them.

Freddie cleared his throat and continued. "Please give Mr and Mrs Harper the St Athelstan's welcome, and help them if they get lost. All right, carry on."

Everyone instantly returned to their previous conversations, and the noise level rose to extra high again.

Freddie came over. "The noise will drop soon, when the boys leave. I know they make a terrible racket, but I don't like them eating in silence. They get precious few times to let loose."

Charlotte nodded, wishing there was a school rule about talking quietly in the refectory. She couldn't remember it being this noisy at school. Then again, that had been such a long time ago.

"I'll grab something to eat," Freddie said. He went off to get his food but was intercepted on the way back by one of the teachers before he could sit down.

Charlotte and Angus finished their fish and chips and went to the dessert counter to choose a pudding. Both opted for profiteroles. Eventually, Freddie returned, sat down with them and began his meal.

A large group of younger boys left and the noise level dropped.

"So," Freddie said, cutting into his fish, "how are you finding the place so far?"

"Impressive," Angus said. "The facilities are excellent."

"The boys seem well-behaved," Charlotte added, aware that several teachers were sitting close enough to hear.

"They're good lads, mostly," Freddie said. "They just need a firm hand now and then."

One of the teachers, a woman in her forties with greying hair, leaned over. "You're the new computing teacher?"

"That's right," Charlotte said.

"Thank goodness. We've been limping along without one for what feels like years. I'm Sarah Hartley, head of science."

"Nice to meet you," Charlotte replied.

They carried on eating and talking when Sarah was mid-sentence about the GCSE science syllabus, and Mr Sandbrook, who Charlotte had gathered was head of geography, let out a long sigh and put down his fork.

"Sorry," he said. "But if I hear one more parent complain about field trips, I'm going to lose it."

Sarah raised her eyebrows. "What's happened now?"

"Mrs Ashworth-Pennington." Sandbrook said the name as if it were a medical diagnosis. "Three-page email. Three pages. About the year 9 Dartmoor trip."

"What was wrong with it?" Charlotte asked.

"Where to start? Her son got mud on his boots. Apparently they were new Christian Dior D-Towns, and she wants the school to pay for replacements." He picked up his fork again and jabbed at his food. "She also said the packed lunches were inadequate because there was no gluten-free option."

"Was her son gluten-free?" Angus asked.

"No. She just thought he should eat less gluten, said it was giving him brain fog."

Charlotte stifled a laugh.

Sarah shook her head. "That's nothing. Last term I had a father ring me at nine o'clock on a Sunday evening to tell me his son should have got a grade nine in his mock exam. When I explained the marking scheme, he said he'd checked the answers on ChatGPT and I was wrong."

"Was he wrong?" Charlotte asked.

"Of course he was wrong. It gave him the answer for a completely different exam board." Sarah took a sip of water. "He then asked if I'd ever considered retraining."

Charlotte glanced at Angus, who was clearly enjoying himself. This was more like it: real teachers, moaning about real things. It reminded her of what Sophie had said about parents being a hundred times worse than the children.

Sandbrook wasn't finished. "The worst are the ones who email at midnight. You know they've had a glass of wine and they're fuming about something trivial. Then you get in the next morning, and there's a fourteen-paragraph essay about why their child should be moved to a different maths set."

"Do you reply?" Charlotte asked.

"God, no." He looked over at Freddie. "Never reply to a parent email sent after six p.m. Wait until morning. Half the time they email again at seven a.m., apologising."

"And the other half?" Angus said.

Sandbrook smiled grimly. "They double down."

Sarah turned to Charlotte. "You'll get it, too, being the

computing teacher. Parents either think their child is the next Bill Gates, and you're holding them back, or they're terrified you'll teach them something dangerous and they'll end up hacking the Bank of England."

Charlotte kept her face neutral. "I'll bear that in mind."

"Just wait until parents' evening," Sandbrook said darkly. "That's when the real fun starts."

They were interrupted by scraping chairs as a number of boys left the canteen quickly, ignoring a teacher's command to walk, not run. A dark-haired boy put his head round the door and beckoned his friends. They got up, dumped their plates on the clearing trolley, and ran out.

A teacher stood up and made for the door, followed by another, and another. Charlotte and Angus exchanged glances. "Something's going down," Angus said.

"Do we follow, or just leave them to it?"

"I'll go and see what's happening." Angus stood up and headed outside.

Charlotte was left sitting with empty plates. Curiosity got the better of her. She got up, put the dirty plates on the trolley, and left.

It was clear immediately what was going on. A large crowd of schoolboys had formed a circle on the field near one of the football goalposts. In the centre, two boys were fighting.

Charlotte was instantly transported back to her childhood. Fights had broken out frequently. It had been part of her education in a dodgy state school in Hemel Hempstead. She'd got in a few scraps herself in her first year at secondary school, but after that she had avoided trouble as much as possible.

She realised she was smiling and pulled her face straight. It wasn't good for a teacher to act as if a fight between pupils was normal. This was a very different time. And although fighting still happened, it was frowned upon much more.

Her two sons, Gethin and Rhys, had had a couple of fights when they were at school, but luckily they'd stayed out of serious trouble most of the time. At least, that's what she hoped was the case.

Some of the teachers pulled boys away to get inside the circle and stop the fight. It took a minute, but eventually two male teachers emerged from the scrum, each holding a boy by the scruff of the neck. Angus was close by, but there was nothing for him to do. The teachers had it under control.

The crowd started to disperse now that the action was over. "All right, everybody, back to the common room," one of the teachers said.

Angus walked over. "Two boys from year 7, apparently."

"What was it about?"

"No idea. They've taken them to Freddie's office."

Charlotte looked at the boys trailing back to the building, some disappointed the entertainment was over, others chatting excitedly about what they'd seen.

"Welcome to St Athelstan's," Angus muttered.

"Quite the first evening," Charlotte replied.

They headed back inside.

CHAPTER 7

After dinner, Charlotte and Angus returned to their apartment. "I thought it would be more formal," Charlotte said, dropping onto the sofa. "It was a bit disappointing."

"You mean you wanted it more like Hogwarts?" Angus smiled.

"I suppose I was expecting that." Charlotte stood up and went over to her computer at the desk, and Angus sat on the sofa.

"If I'd known how bad the furniture would be," said Charlotte, "I'd have brought some throws. I could still order some on the internet. They have mail and deliveries here."

"Best not. Remember, we're supposed to be impoverished teachers."

Charlotte wrinkled her nose. "If we go off-site, I'll get some."

"What are you doing, anyway?" Angus asked. "Hacking the school Wi-Fi already?"

"I don't need to: I have the password. Although it's ridiculously unsafe. School123 is not a good password, especially for the staff Wi-Fi."

"There's a separate staff Wi-Fi?"

"Yes. There's a public one that anyone can use, and a staff one, which is meant to be encrypted. Can't see much difference between the two at the moment, though. I'm just having a look around the servers now." Charlotte's fingers moved across the keyboard. "There's not much here, just a few folders for each member of staff. They each have their own area. Nothing of note so far. Although ... hang on a minute. What's this?"

Angus pulled out his phone and checked his messages.

"This is interesting," Charlotte said, leaning closer to the screen. "There's an encrypted hard disk on the server. It's hidden too."

"If it's hidden, how come you can see it?"

Charlotte turned around and gave him a look.

"All right, all right. Of course you can see it, because *you* know where to look."

"Exactly. I like a challenge. I'm going to decrypt this."

"How long will that take?"

"No idea. I'll start now."

There was a knock on the door. Angus opened it to find Freddie standing there, looking even more exhausted than he had earlier.

"Sorry about all that at dinner," Freddie said. "The boys are getting very restless. There's a lot of tension at the moment. We need to get it sorted."

Angus invited him in, and Charlotte turned her chair to face them.

Freddie handed them each a sheet of paper. "These are your timetables. Breakfast is at seven forty-five, same place as tonight, and lunch is from one till two. Twice a week you're needed for playground duty."

They looked at their timetables.

"Angus, you'll be helping Mr Franks for the first couple of days. He's the current PE teacher. Shadow him, get a feel for things, then you're on your own. He's taking some sick leave due to stress, but I've asked him to stay on a few days to get you settled in. I've built in a few gaps in your timetable so that you have time to investigate."

He turned to Charlotte. "You'll be on your own from the start, I'm afraid. I've been recruiting for a computing teacher for the last eighteen months. Nothing."

Charlotte nodded. "I understand."

"If there's anything you need, any time, just ask. You can get me on WhatsApp."

"What time are you up, usually?" Angus asked.

"Early."

"Fancy a run in the morning? You can show me the best routes. Might help with the stress."

Freddie hesitated, then nodded. "All right, I'll knock for you at six."

"Perfect."

When Freddie left, Charlotte refocused on her computer. "He seems stressed beyond belief."

"Indeed. Having a pupil in hospital, probably due to bullying or something worse..."

"We'll get to the bottom of it," Charlotte said, her eyes fixed on the screen. "Then things can go back to normal. Or as normal as it gets at a private school in an old building in the middle of Devon."

"Makes me yearn for my state comprehensive," said Angus.

Charlotte didn't reply. She was already absorbed in the encrypted drive, lines of code scrolling across her screen.

Angus watched her for a moment, then stood up and stretched. "I'm getting ready for bed," he said. "Early start tomorrow."

"Mmm," Charlotte murmured, not looking up.

"Charlotte."

"What?"

"Don't stay up all night."

She glanced at him. "I won't. I just want to get a sense of what I'm dealing with."

Angus knew that meant she'd be at it for hours, but there was no point arguing. When Charlotte was onto something, she didn't let go.

He left her to it and headed for the bathroom.

CHAPTER 8

The next morning, Charlotte woke to the sound of Angus moving quietly around the flat. She checked her phone: five forty-five. He'd be going on his run with Freddie soon.

"Morning," she mumbled, rubbing her eyes.

"Morning. Go back to sleep. You were up past midnight."

"Was I?" Charlotte had lost track of time working on the encrypted drive. She'd made some progress, but it was heavily protected. Whoever had set it up knew what they were doing.

"Yes. Coffee's on if you want it."

"Thanks."

Angus left for his run and Charlotte dragged herself out of bed. She had her first lesson at nine: year 7 computing. A class of eleven- and twelve-year-olds. The thought of it made her nervous again. She showered and dressed in what she hoped was sensible teacher clothing: black trousers, a plain blouse, flat shoes.

At breakfast, Charlotte and Angus joined the staff table. Most of the teachers from the night before were there, plus a few new faces. Sarah Hartley, the head of science, waved them over.

"Morning! How was your first night? Did you sleep all right?"

"No, bad, thanks," Charlotte said, sitting down with her plate. "Took a while to get used to the sounds. Old buildings creak a lot."

"You get used to it. After a week you won't even notice." Sarah took a sip of tea. "So, how long have you two been married?"

"Four years," Charlotte said.

"Five," Angus said, at exactly the same moment.

Sarah raised her eyebrows.

Angus recovered first. "Nearly five. It'll be five in the spring."

"March," Charlotte added, a beat too late.

"That's sweet. Where did you get married? It's an unusual month to do it. Did you go abroad?"

"Registry office," they both said. At least they agreed on that.

"And the honeymoon?"

"The Lake District," Charlotte said.

"Cornwall," Angus said, simultaneously.

Another silence. Sandbrook, the geography teacher, paused mid-chew and glanced between them.

"We went to both, didn't we, darling?" Angus's smile was stiff but convincing enough. "Cornwall first, then up to the Lakes. A sort of touring honeymoon."

Charlotte nodded. "That's right. Both."

"Lovely," Sarah said, though she didn't sound entirely convinced. "My husband and I went to Crete. Food poisoning on day three. Spent the rest of the week in the hotel bathroom. Very romantic."

They managed the rest of breakfast without further incident, though Charlotte noticed Sandbrook giving them an odd glance as he left.

In the corridor afterwards, Angus pulled Charlotte into an alcove. "Four years?"

"I miscounted."

"You miscounted our fake marriage? We agreed five. In the car. I was driving and you were making notes on your phone."

"I forgot."

"You forgot how long we've been married. And the Lake District? We agreed Cornwall."

Charlotte shrugged. "I've always wanted to go to the Lake District. It just came out."

"It just came out? We rehearsed this, Charlotte."

"Fine, fine. I got flustered. She put me on the spot."

"She asked where we went on our honeymoon. That's not exactly an interrogation."

Charlotte pressed her fingers to her temples.

"Right. From now on, we went to Cornwall for our honeymoon. We've been married for five years. We got married in March at a registry office. If anyone asks anything else, say you can't remember and change the subject. Understood?"

"Yes, got it. What if they ask what our first dance was? Oooh, it was to 'At Last' by Etta James."

"Why Etta James?"

"Because it's what everyone picks and no one will question it."

Angus straightened his tie. "I'd have picked 'You Do Something to Me' by Paul Weller."

Charlotte's expression softened. "You've been thinking about our wedding song?"

Angus opened his mouth to reply, but Freddie appeared at the end of the corridor and gestured for them to follow him. "Come on, I'll introduce you to a few more people."

He led them down another corridor and into a smaller

room that looked like a staff common area. A few teachers were scattered about: some doing marking, others chatting over cups of tea.

"Bryony," Freddie called.

A woman in her mid-thirties looked up from a laptop. She was elegant, dressed in a sharp navy suit, her blonde hair pulled back in a sleek bun. She closed the laptop and stood up, her expression neutral.

"This is Miss James, our deputy head," Freddie said. "Bryony, meet Jack and Bridget Harper, our new PE and computing teachers."

Miss James extended a hand. "Welcome to St Athelstan's. I hope you'll settle in quickly. We're really glad you're here to help sort out more than one problem." Charlotte knew her meaning straight away: she was the one person whom Freddie had told the truth. The one who knew they weren't really teachers.

"Thank you," Charlotte said.

"If you need anything, my office is on the first floor. Though I'm sure Freddie's already given you the tour."

"He has," Angus said. "Very thorough."

"Good." Miss James picked up her laptop. "I'll see you around." She nodded to Freddie and left.

"She's efficient," Freddie said, watching her go. "Runs a tight ship. The school would fall apart without her."

He led them over to a man sitting in an armchair by the window, a stack of essays on his lap. He was in his forties, with thinning hair and wire-rimmed glasses. He looked up as they approached.

"Morning, David," Freddie said. "Jack, Bridget, this is Mr Brooke, head of English. David, meet Jack and Bridget Harper."

Mr Brooke stayed seated. "Oh, hello! Yes, hello. Welcome." His eyes darted between them and Freddie, as if he were worried he'd said something wrong.

"Nice to meet you," Angus said.

"Yes, yes. Likewise. Computing and PE, isn't it? Excellent. We need all the help we can get." He laughed nervously. "Always good to have fresh faces."

"David looks after the Coleridge House boys," Freddie said.

"I do. Coleridge, good house. Good boys, mostly. Well, I won't keep you. Lots to do before the meeting." He looked down at his essays, though Charlotte noticed he didn't appear to be reading them.

"Is he all right?" Charlotte asked quietly as they moved away.

"He's been on edge lately," Freddie muttered. "Like a lot of the staff. That's part of why you're here."

They crossed the room to where an older woman was pouring herself a cup of tea from a large urn. She was in her sixties, stocky, with short grey hair and a no-nonsense air about her. She wore a name badge: "Mrs Hodge, Matron."

"Mrs Hodge," Freddie said. "Got a minute?"

She turned, holding her cup of tea.

"Meet Jack and Bridget Harper. Jack's our new PE teacher; Bridget's taking over computing."

Mrs Hodge shook their hands. Her grip was strong. "Hello. I run the medical room. If any of the boys get hurt, or if *you* get hurt, you come to me. I've been here ten years and I've seen it all. Twisted ankles, broken noses, the odd case of appendicitis. COVID was a breeze, compared to what I usually have to deal with." She looked at Charlotte. "You'll do fine, love. Just don't trust everything you hear."

Charlotte blinked. "Excuse me?"

Mrs Hodge took a sip of tea. "This place has a lot of gossip. Teachers talk. Boys talk. Not all of it's true. Use your own judgement."

"Right," Charlotte said. "I'll keep that in mind."

Mrs Hodge nodded. "Good. Now, if you'll excuse me, I've

got a boy with a headache waiting for me. Probably just needs to hydrate. Nice to meet you both." She walked out, cup of tea in hand.

Angus watched her go. "She's interesting."

"She doesn't miss much," Freddie said. "Sharp as a tack. If anyone knows what's really going on in this school, it's her."

"Should we talk to her?" Charlotte asked quietly.

"Maybe," Freddie said. "But carefully. She's loyal to the school, but she's also loyal to the boys. If she thinks you're here to cause trouble, she won't help you."

Charlotte glanced at Angus. Mrs Hodge could be useful – but Freddie was right. They'd need to tread carefully.

CHAPTER 9

At eight forty-five, Charlotte made her way to the computer suite. It was on the second floor, along a corridor lined with science labs. The door was labelled "ICT Suite."

She unlocked it and stepped inside.

The room was crisp and clean, painted white, with a large screen and a digital projector at the front. To the left was a whiteboard.

Charlotte pulled out her bag of whiteboard markers and a wiper she'd brought from home. The teacher's desk was at the front, positioned so that she could see all the computers. Rows of monitors stretched back, twenty in total, arranged in pairs.

Charlotte sat down at the desk and logged into her teacher account. She'd logged on the night before and discovered she had the same access to the network as every other teacher. A bit disappointing, but then she'd enjoyed the challenge of hacking the network administrator's account. That had been a bit of fun which hadn't taken long.

She pulled up the lesson plan Sophie had given her. It was the first lesson of a six-week unit on how the internet worked.

Charlotte skimmed through it and sighed. It was incredibly dry. Packets, protocols, IP addresses. All important, sure, but hardly exciting for eleven-year-olds. Surely it would be better to get them coding?

She opened a new tab and searched for a Python tutorial site. Yes, that's what she'd do. Forget the boring curriculum: she'd teach them something useful.

The first pupil arrived, a small boy with dark hair and glasses. "Hello, miss." He headed straight to one of the computers at the back.

Another boy arrived a moment later. He was taller, with blond hair. He stared at Charlotte, then went to the back of the room and sat next to the first boy.

The first boy was already logging on. A moment later, an online game loaded on his screen. The second boy did the same.

Charlotte wasn't sure what the school rules were about playing games. She didn't say anything to start with, but she made a mental note that if they didn't shut down the games when she started teaching, she'd deal with it. Suddenly, everything Sophie had told her about taking command of the room had disappeared from her mind.

More boys trickled in. By five to nine, there were eighteen students. A lot fewer than at her sons' state school, where thirty to a class had been the norm. All of them had logged in and immediately opened either a game or YouTube.

Charlotte stood at the front and took a deep breath. She was the teacher. She was the one in charge. She had to take control and make sure these young minds got the education they deserved – and which their parents were paying for.

"Right, everyone," she said.

A couple of boys looked up, but most carried on staring at their screens.

Luckily Charlotte remembered one thing Sophie had told her: give clear, simple instructions.

"Hello, everyone. I'm Mrs Harper, and I want you to close your games and your YouTube videos, then turn around and listen." She said it in a clear teacher voice, firm but not shouting.

Slowly, the boys turned around and closed the programs. A couple at the side carried on staring at their screens.

"Hey, you two. I told you to close that down."

One of the boys clicked the X on his window and turned round. The other followed reluctantly.

"Thank you."

Eighteen pairs of eyes watched Charlotte. Some looked curious. Others looked bored already.

"Right. As I said, I'm Mrs Harper, and I'm your new computing teacher. Luckily for you, I have lots of real-life computing experience, and I'm going to teach you the things you really need to know."

One of the boys in the front row put his hand up.

"Yes?" said Charlotte.

"Will you teach us how to hack into things?"

A few boys sniggered. Charlotte kept her face neutral. "I'd love to," she said. "Unfortunately, though, I don't think the UK government, the headmaster, or your parents would be very happy with me if I did."

A couple of the boys groaned. Charlotte ignored them. "However, one of the most important skills you can have, if you want to learn how to *ethically* hack when you've left school, is programming. So that's what we're going to do."

One of the boys' hands shot up. "I did Scratch, miss."

Charlotte cringed inwardly. Scratch was a block-based programming language mainly used by younger children. Colourful blocks which you dragged around to make things happen.

"That's great," she said. "Today, though, we're going to use a text-based language called Python. It's been used to build all sorts of things: Instagram, Spotify, X, even parts of ChatGPT."

The boys all stared at her. She wasn't sure if they were enthralled or ambivalent.

"Open a web browser," she said, "and we'll use an online Python editor."

The boys turned back to their computers. Some opened browsers immediately. Others looked confused.

Charlotte walked around the room. "If you don't know how to open a browser, just double-click on the browser icon."

A few boys nodded and followed her instructions.

"Right," Charlotte said, returning to the front. "Go to this website." She wrote the URL on the whiteboard in large letters. "It's a free Python editor. You don't need to sign up or anything."

The boys typed in the address. Slowly, the website loaded on their screens.

"Okay," Charlotte said. "Who here has written any code before? Apart from Scratch."

Three hands went up.

"Good. For those of you who haven't, don't worry. Programming is basically giving instructions to a computer. You tell it what to do, step by step, and it does it. Simple."

One of the boys at the back muttered, "Doesn't sound simple."

Charlotte smiled. "It's not as hard as you think. We'll start with the basics. The first thing you learn in any programming language is how to make the computer say something. In Python, we use a command called print."

She turned to the whiteboard and wrote: *print("Hello, world!")*

"This is your first line of code," she said. "Copy this exactly into the editor on your screen. Make sure you include the brackets and the quotation marks."

The boys started typing. Charlotte walked around the

room, checking their progress. A few had made mistakes: leaving out quotation marks, using the wrong brackets. She corrected them patiently.

"Once you've typed it in," she said, "press the Run button. It's the green one at the top of the page."

One by one, the boys pressed Run. Their screens displayed *Hello, world!*

A few of them grinned.

"There you go," Charlotte said. "You've just written your first program."

"That's it?" one boy said, sounding disappointed.

"That's the start," Charlotte said. "Now we're going to make it more interesting. Delete what you've written and type this instead."

She wrote on the whiteboard:

name = input("What's your name?")

print("Hello, " + name + "!")

"This program will ask for your name, then say hello to you," Charlotte explained. "The first line creates a variable called *name* and stores whatever you type. The second line prints a message using that variable."

The boys typed it in, more confident now. A few made mistakes, but Charlotte helped them.

"Now run it," she said.

The boys pressed Run. A prompt appeared on their screens: *What's your name?*

They typed in their names. A moment later, the screen displayed: *Hello, James! Hello, Tom!* or whatever name they'd entered.

The room filled with excited chatter.

"Miss, can I make it say something else?"

"Miss, what if I want it to ask more questions?"

Charlotte smiled. This was going better than she'd expected. "Okay, settle down," she said. "Yes, you can make it say anything you want. Try changing the message. Instead of 'Hello', make it say something funny."

The boys got to work. A few minutes later, one boy raised his hand. "Miss, mine says, 'You smell, Tom!'"

The class erupted in laughter.

"Very mature," Charlotte said, but she couldn't help smiling.

Charlotte saw two boys giggling at a screen and walked over. On the screen was written "Your mum smells."

She rolled her eyes. "All right, let's move on. Who wants to learn how to make the computer do maths?"

Most of the hands went up.

Charlotte spent the next thirty minutes walking them through basic operations: addition, subtraction, multiplication. She showed them how to create a simple calculator that asked for two numbers and added them together.

The boys were engaged now. Even the ones who'd looked bored at the start were typing away, trying things out.

With ten minutes left, Charlotte set them a challenge. "Right, now I want you to create a program that asks for your name and your age, then tells you how old you'll be in ten years. Use what we've learned so far."

The boys got to work. Charlotte walked around the room, helping those who were stuck. A few figured it out quickly, while others needed more guidance. But by the end of the lesson, most of them had working programs.

"Okay, everyone, save your work by copying it into a text file on your folder," Charlotte said. "We'll continue this next lesson. Well done today. You've all done brilliantly."

The bell rang. The boys logged off and filed out.

Charlotte sat down at the desk and exhaled. Her first lesson was over. And it had actually gone well.

"Miss?"

She looked up. It was the small boy with glasses who had

arrived first. He was approaching her desk nervously. "Yes?" she said.

"Can I ... can I work on this at home too? I want to try making something more complicated."

Charlotte smiled. "Of course. The website is free, and you can use it as much as you like. The best way to become a good programmer is to practise as much as you can."

"Thanks, miss." He hesitated, then added quietly, "Miss, do you know how Oliver is? The boy who's in hospital?"

Charlotte's attention sharpened, and she kept her voice casual with an effort. "I've heard he's going to be okay. Do you know him?"

The boy nodded. "He's my brother's friend. They're both in year 11. My brother's really worried about him."

"I'm sure he'll be fine," Charlotte said gently. "What has your brother said about him?"

The boy shifted his weight. "Just that Oliver changed this term. He used to be really fun and into music, then he went all serious and secretive. He wouldn't talk to anyone properly. My brother asked him what was wrong, but Oliver just said he was busy doing important stuff."

Charlotte nodded, keeping her expression neutral. "That must be worrying for your brother."

"Yeah. He thinks it's because Oliver joined a club or something. But Oliver wouldn't say."

"A club?"

The boy shrugged. "I don't know. Just something my brother said. Anyway, thanks for the lesson, miss. It was really good." He gave her a quick smile and left.

Charlotte sat back in her chair. *A club.* Oliver had changed this term. Become secretive. Then ended up in hospital after a suicide attempt, or possibly something even more sinister.

She pulled out her phone and texted Angus: *Need to talk. Got something.*

After her first lesson, she needed a coffee, so made her

way to the staffroom. On her way, she looked out of the window and saw a skip filled with rubbish. She made her way outside for a closer look. In the corner was a pile of old dial telephones, a box of headphones with curly cords, several language lab tape recorders, a broken PA system amplifier, a set of multimeters from the physics department, and a stack of circuit boards pulled from the school's old intercom system.

She had a perfect idea.

CHAPTER 10

While Charlotte was inside teaching coding, Angus was outside on the sports field with a group of teenagers: year 11 pupils, aged fifteen and sixteen.

They'd got changed and met him outside the changing rooms, ready for exercise. Angus had checked them off on the register Mr Franks had given him. Eighteen boys, all present. Mr Franks himself had introduced Angus as "Mr Harper, who'll be covering for me," then gone back inside. Angus suspected he'd gone straight to the staffroom for a quiet sit-down.

"Right, lads," he said, clapping his hands together. "Football today. But first, warm-up. Two laps of the pitch, then some stretches."

A few groans, but they set off jogging. Angus jogged with them, keeping pace at the back to make sure no one slacked off. The air was crisp, the grass still damp with morning dew. It felt good to be outside, moving, rather than stuck in a stuffy office or classroom.

Once they'd finished the laps, Angus led them through stretches – hamstrings, quads, calves. Sophie's notes had been thorough. He'd memorised the basics, and the boys seemed to know the drill anyway.

"All right, now we're going to work on some skills," he said. "Dribbling, passing, control. Split into pairs."

The boys paired off without fuss. Angus handed out footballs and set them to work dribbling between cones, passing back and forth, controlling the ball with different parts of their feet. He walked among them, offering corrections, encouragement, the odd bit of advice.

It was easier than he'd expected. The boys were focused, engaged. Football did that, he supposed. Even the ones who weren't particularly sporty seemed to enjoy it.

He mused on how different teenage boys were to teenage girls. His daughter, Grace, the result of his marriage to Rhona, was his pride and joy. However, her teenage years had been difficult at times. Worry over having a teenage girl, and all the threats that potentially posed, had been the cause of many sleepless nights. But in the end, she'd turned out well: confident, independent, sensible.

Boys were different. Louder, more physical, less complicated in some ways. Or maybe that was just his perception.

He felt a bit like Ted Lasso, standing on the sidelines, watching the boys practise. Football had never been his favourite sport – he was more of a runner – but it was massively popular among young and old alike. So far, the boys had behaved themselves. He'd wondered if sport this early in the morning would mean laziness and misbehaviour, but not so far. Was being a teacher meant to be this easy? He wondered how Charlotte was getting on.

He looked up at the sky. Dark clouds were moving in their direction and he felt a spot of rain.

"Right, lads, let's wrap up the drills," he called. "We'll play matches for the last twenty minutes. Two pitches, split yourselves into two teams of five and two teams of four."

The boys didn't need telling twice. They divided themselves quickly with no arguments or fuss and set up goals using cones.

Angus refereed one pitch, keeping an eye on the other.

The rain started to come down properly, but the boys didn't seem to care. If anything, they played harder, sliding in the mud, laughing when someone slipped.

Angus blew the whistle. "Last five minutes!"

One of the boys, tall and confident, was clearly the best player. He dribbled past two defenders and kicked the ball neatly into the goal.

His teammates cheered. "Nice one, Harrison!" someone shouted.

Mark Harrison grinned as he jogged back to the halfway line. Angus made a mental note of the name. Always useful to know who the natural leaders were.

Harrison had just scored again when another boy, shorter and red-faced, shoved him hard from behind. "Stop showing off, you arsehole!"

Harrison whipped round. "What's your problem, Davies?"

"You think you're so special, don't you? Just because Brooke picked you—"

Angus blew the whistle sharply. "Hey! Break it up there!"

Davies backed off, but his face was still twisted with anger. "It's not fair. Oliver was better than him, and look what happened to him."

Harrison went very still. "Shut up about Oliver."

"Why? Everyone knows what—"

"I said shut up!" Harrison looked genuinely shaken.

Angus stepped between them. "That's enough, both of you. Davies, sit out. Harrison, take a breather."

Davies sloped off to the sidelines, muttering under his breath. Harrison stood for a moment, hands on his hips, staring at the ground. Then he jogged back to his position without a word.

Angus watched them both carefully. *Brooke picked you. Oliver was better*. Whatever was going on in this school, it involved some kind of selection process. And from the looks of it, being chosen or not being chosen came with consequences.

As the game continued, Angus noticed two boys on the sidelines, standing apart. One was small and slight, the other stockier, and both looked uncomfortable. They weren't injured, just reluctant.

Angus walked over. "Everything all right, you two?"

The smaller boy shrugged. "We're not really into football, sir."

"Fair enough," Angus said, "but you still need to participate. How about you two help me out by being linesmen on the other pitch? Watch for the ball going out and call it when it does."

The boys looked relieved. "Okay, sir."

It was a small thing, but it would keep them involved without forcing them to do something they hated. Angus remembered one of his friends being that kid at school: the one who dreaded PE, who always got picked last. He wasn't going to be the teacher who made it worse.

He checked his watch and blew the whistle for full time. The boys groaned, then trudged off the pitches, muddy and soaking wet, but in good spirits.

"Right, get yourselves showered and changed," Angus said. "Well done today. Good effort."

They filed into the changing rooms. Angus waited outside with Mr Franks, who had reappeared just as they were leaving the field.

"How'd it go?" Mr Franks asked.

"Fine. They're a good group."

"They are. Year 11s usually are. It's the year 9s you need to watch out for. Full of hormones and attitude." He lit a cigarette, and Angus tried to keep his face neutral. Surely there must be a rule about not smoking on the school grounds? "You settling in all right?" He blew the smoke to the side.

"Yeah. Still finding my feet, I suppose. I only got here yesterday, so that's to be expected."

Mr Franks nodded. "It's a good school. Bit strange lately, though. Staff leaving, that business with the boy in hospital. Makes you wonder what's really going on."

Angus kept his tone casual. "Yeah, I heard about that. What happened?"

Franks shrugged. "No one really knows. Boy tried to top himself, apparently. Oliver Sutherland. Quiet lad, into music. Last person you'd expect." He took a drag of his cigarette. "His mates reckoned he'd been acting weird for a few weeks. Secretive, you know? Then this."

"That's rough."

"Yeah. Anyway, best not dwell on it. You've got Year 9 next, right?"

"Year 8."

"Good luck with that." Franks gave him a grim smile and walked off.

Angus stood for a moment, thinking. *Oliver had been acting secretively.*

The changing-room door opened, and the boys started to emerge, hair damp, shirts untucked, ties askew. They headed towards the main building, chatting and shoving each other.

Angus waited until they'd all left, then walked into the changing room for a quick check. Wet towels were on the floor, along with a forgotten water bottle. He made a mental note: *remind the next class to tidy up after themselves.*

As he locked the door, his phone buzzed. A text, from Charlotte: *Need to talk. Got something.*

He replied: *Same. Meet at lunch?*

Yes.

Angus pocketed his phone and headed for the school building. One lesson down, several more to go. But already they were starting to get somewhere.

CHAPTER 11

At lunchtime Angus went to the front of the queue for food, his mind turning over the morning's events. The altercation between Davies and Harrison had kept replaying in his head. *Brooke picked you. Oliver was better.* It had to mean something.

He grabbed a plateful of pasta and looked around for Charlotte, but she was nowhere to be seen. He found a seat at the staff table and tucked in. The food was good quality, though the portions were small. He wondered how growing boys who needed three thousand calories a day managed with such small servings. No wonder they were always hungry.

He was almost finished when he saw Charlotte appear in the refectory doorway and pause, scanning the room. He raised his hand and she hurried over. Her face was like thunder, which did not bode well.

Instead of queuing for food, she came straight over and sat down next to him. "My laptop's been stolen," she muttered.

Angus put down his fork. "Wait, what?"

"My laptop's been stolen," she repeated, her voice low but

furious.

"From our flat?"

"Yes. I don't think anything else has gone."

For the first time in a long time, Angus wanted to swear. He restrained himself. "That's ... not good."

"I know. Someone's gone into our flat and rifled through our things."

"Is it password protected?"

"Of course it is."

"So they won't be able to get anything off it?"

She shook her head. "I don't think so. It's encrypted. But still..."

"Was there any sign of a break-in? I mean, we're on the first floor, so they must have gone through the main door. Who has keys?"

Charlotte shrugged. "Who knows? It's an old building. Lots of people have lived in that flat before us. There could be dozens of keys floating around."

"Have you told Freddie?"

"Not yet. I wanted to tell you first."

Angus leaned closer. "Weren't you using that laptop to try and decrypt the hidden drive on the network?"

"That's exactly what I was doing."

"Was there anything on it that could get you into trouble?"

She stared at him. "Of course not. I'm not stupid. I knew there was a chance the laptop could get stolen. It's basically a burner laptop. Everything important is backed up elsewhere, and there are minimal installations on it."

"Okay. You should go and tell Freddie. Or do you want lunch first?"

Charlotte shook her head. "I'm not hungry." She stood up and headed off.

Angus finished his pasta, his mind racing. This was not good. How safe were they in a place where pupils were being hurt and someone could just walk into their flat and take whatever they wanted?

This is brazen, he thought. Whoever had done it wasn't trying to hide the fact. They'd done it on purpose, to spook them.

There was no way someone would run the risk of stealing a laptop from a teacher's flat just to use it. They were trying to find out what Charlotte and Angus were doing there. Which meant someone suspected them of being something other than a pair of new teachers.

Angus stood up and headed straight for the headmaster's office, but it was empty. Then he checked the field, but there was no sign of Freddie. He tried the staffroom next, but he wasn't there either.

Where the hell was he?

Angus was heading back to the refectory when he spotted Charlotte and Freddie coming down the corridor. Both looked grim.

"We're calling an assembly," Freddie said. "Right now."

"Is that a good idea?" Angus asked. "Won't it draw attention to us?"

"Someone's already drawn attention to you by stealing the laptop," Freddie said. "We need to make it clear that this won't be tolerated."

Half an hour later, a special assembly had been called. The whole school filed into the main hall. Rows of boys in navy blazers sat on chairs, staff standing at the sides. The noise was deafening until Freddie stepped onto the stage. Then silence fell immediately.

"A serious crime has been committed this morning," Freddie said, his voice carrying across the hall. "Mrs Harper's laptop has been stolen from her flat. Whoever has taken it, you have one hour to return it. No further action will be taken if the item is returned within that time. However, if the laptop is not returned, and I find out who has done this, the consequence will be immediate expulsion. This is a prestigious school, and we do not tolerate this sort of behaviour. If necessary, the police will be called. I sincerely hope this will not be necessary."

Angus stood at the side of the hall, his eyes scanning the room. The older boys sat near the back. A few looked uncomfortable. Others stared straight ahead, expressionless. He wouldn't rule out the teachers either. There must be at least one who had a key to their flat.

As the boys filed out, Angus checked his watch. One hour, during which most of the boys would be in lessons. If someone was going to return the laptop, they'd have to do it soon.

Charlotte approached him after the hall had cleared, and Freddie joined them. "Don't worry, I'll get to the bottom of this," he said.

"But what about our flat?" Charlotte asked. "There was no sign of a break-in. Someone must have a key."

"I know. I've called a locksmith to change the lock, and they'll be here later. In the meantime, make sure you bolt the door from the inside when you're in there. Do you have anything else of value?"

"It's not so much that the laptop was valuable," Charlotte murmured. "I was using it to look at the school network. There's an encrypted hard disk on the network, which I think is highly suspicious. I was using the laptop to try and get into it."

Freddie frowned. "An encrypted hard disk?"

"Yes."

"We must get your laptop back. I can't have the computer network being used for illicit purposes."

"What sort of thing could an encrypted drive contain?" Angus asked. "Or is that something we shouldn't know?"

"It could be anything or nothing," Charlotte replied. "If I can get into it, I'll know for sure."

"Have you found anything else suspicious about the computer system?" Freddie asked.

"Not yet, but I won't be able to get any further without my laptop. If mine doesn't turn up, I'll get another one delivered later today."

"Thank you. I'll keep you posted." Freddie nodded to them both and left.

Angus turned to Charlotte. "Other than the laptop being stolen, how was your first morning?"

Charlotte's face softened slightly. "It was fine. Harder than I thought it would be, but overall it was quite enjoyable. I'm teaching them all to code. That's what I've decided to do while I'm here."

"Good. Mine went okay, too, though..." He paused. "This is what I meant to tell you before we got sidetracked by the laptop. Two boys got into a fight during football, and one of them said something about Mr Brooke picking students. And he also mentioned Oliver."

Charlotte's eyes narrowed. "Mr Brooke?"

"Yeah. The boy said something like, 'You think you're so special just because Brooke picked you.' And then he mentioned Oliver was better."

"Better at what?"

"I don't know. But whatever it is, it involves some kind of selection. And it's connected to Oliver."

Charlotte nodded. "One of my students said something similar. Oliver changed this term, became secretive. His friend, this student's older brother, thinks he joined some kind of club."

"A club run by Brooke?"

"Maybe."

They stood in silence for a moment.

"We need to find out more about Mr Brooke," Charlotte said.

"Agreed. But we have to be careful. If he's behind this, he's dangerous."

Half an hour later, Charlotte was in the computer room with her next class when Freddie knocked on the door and beckoned her out.

"Your laptop's been returned," he said, holding it up.

Charlotte's relief lasted about a second. The laptop had been smashed. The casing was dented and cracked, as though it had been run over by a car. When she opened it, the screen was shattered.

"Bastards," she muttered.

Freddie handed it to her. "I'm sorry. Whoever did this clearly wanted to send a message."

Charlotte stared at the ruined laptop. "Message received."

CHAPTER 12

Grigore arrived three hours later. Charlotte met him in the main entrance, where he stood in a hi-vis courier jacket, holding a large box marked with a delivery company logo. He looked the part: clipboard in hand, baseball cap pulled low. "Package for Mrs Harper," he said formally, his accent barely noticeable.

Charlotte signed the fake delivery form and took the box. It was heavier than she'd expected. "Thanks."

Grigore glanced around the entrance hall, checking no one was within earshot, then dropped his voice. "You need protection while you're here?"

"Don't worry, Angus will look after me."

Grigore stared at her for a moment, his expression serious.

"What?"

"He is good man. But if zomeone determined, zey could hurt you both."

"They're more likely to be after both of us, not just me. I have to say, it's disconcerting. I'll be much happier when we get to the bottom of what's going on."

Grigore's gaze swept the entrance hall again, taking in the portraits of stern-faced headmasters, the sweeping staircase, the boys passing in their navy blazers. "This place, it has secrets. Old buildings always do. Be careful."

"I will. Thanks for bringing this so quickly."

"Helena packed extra equipment. Cameras, spare charger, portable hard drive. Everything you need. And she says to call if you need anyzing. Anyzing at all."

"Tell her I will."

Grigore nodded once, adjusted his cap, and left.

Charlotte watched him go, then carried the box back to their flat. Inside, she unpacked it carefully. As promised, Helena had thought of everything: not just a replacement laptop, but tiny cameras, a backup drive, cables, even a portable Wi-Fi hotspot. Charlotte smiled. Helena was nothing if not thorough.

She set up the new laptop on the desk, plugged it in, and got back to work on the encrypted drive.

That night, Charlotte slept better than she'd expected. The cameras Grigore had delivered were now discreetly positioned. One was angled towards the door, the other covering the main room. The extra bolt on the door helped too. She knew her watch would alert her if anyone tried to break in – and if they did, she'd be prepared. Angus had brought a couple of hockey sticks from the PE cupboard and placed them by the bed.

Charlotte looked at them. "Hockey sticks?"

"Just in case."

"In case of what? A midnight hockey tournament?"

"In case someone comes through that door. We've already had a laptop stolen and a threatening note. I'd rather have something in hand than nothing."

Charlotte sat on the edge of the bed. "Angus, we're in a school, not a war zone. The door's bolted, we've got cameras, and my watch will alert me if anyone comes near. You're overreacting."

"I'd rather overreact than under-react." He picked up one

of the sticks and leaned it against the bedside table on his side. "This one's mine. That one's yours."

"I'm not sleeping with a hockey stick."

"It's not in the bed. It's next to it. Just leave it there. Humour me."

Charlotte rolled her eyes but didn't move the stick.

She lay in the darkness, listening to the unfamiliar sounds of the school at night. Distant footsteps in the corridor. A door closing somewhere. The creak of old floorboards. It was strange sleeping somewhere that wasn't home. But Angus was beside her, his breathing slow and steady.

She shifted closer and he stirred slightly, his arm moving around her. But she could tell from the tension in his body that he wasn't asleep yet. He was thinking. Planning.

"Stop planning escape routes and go to sleep," she murmured.

"I'm not planning escape routes."

"Yes you are. I can tell."

He was quiet for a moment. "The fire exit at the end of our corridor leads to the courtyard. From there it's about forty seconds to the car park if we run."

"Goodnight, Angus."

"The car keys are in my coat pocket. Left side."

"Goodnight."

He fell silent.

After a few minutes, Angus's breathing had finally slowed. He always fell asleep so quickly once he let go, which was both admirable and annoying. Since her perimenopause had started, sleep had become harder and harder. But tonight, exhaustion won out. She closed her eyes and let herself drift off.

The hockey stick stood untouched by the bed. She hoped it would stay that way.

CHAPTER 13

Charlotte had another set of new students in the morning lessons: year 8, this time. She gave the same lesson – programming, using Python. It should have been tedious to repeat the same introduction, the same exercises. Instead, she found herself enjoying it. She wanted to start these children on their programming journey and get them excited about code the way she was.

One boy was particularly enthusiastic boy. Instead of heading for the seats near the back, like most of the class, he sat as close as he could to Charlotte's desk.

He pulled out his own laptop, a sleek, expensive-looking model. "Do you mind if I use my own computer, miss?"

Charlotte wasn't sure if that was allowed, but she nodded. "Go ahead."

The boy grinned and opened his laptop, already loading the Python editor before she'd even finished explaining the task to the rest of the class. His fingers moved quickly over the keyboard, confident and practised. She'd have to give him something more challenging to keep him engaged.

"What's your name?" she asked.

"Daniel, miss. Daniel Brooke."

Charlotte's stomach tightened. The same surname as Mr Brooke, the housemaster. Coincidence, or family?

"Any relation to Mr Brooke?" she asked lightly.

"He's my uncle."

Of course he was.

"Right," Charlotte said. "Well, Daniel, since you're already ahead, I've got a challenge for you later. Something a bit more advanced."

Daniel's eyes lit up. "Thanks, miss."

Charlotte started the lesson, but her mind was on Brooke's nephew.

After the lesson ended, and the boys filed out, Charlotte pulled up the student records on her computer. She navigated to Daniel's file. His parents were listed as being abroad: his father working in Singapore, his mother accompanying him. Guardian: David Brooke, uncle. So Daniel lived with him full time.

She was about to close the file when something else caught her eye. A note in the system log: *Library computer access: extended privileges, approved by D. Brooke.*

Charlotte frowned. She opened the school's network monitoring system, the one she'd been given admin access to. She searched for the library computers and looked at the access logs from the past month.

There had been multiple late-evening logins from Library Terminal 3. One of those sessions had accessed the encrypted drive. The same drive she'd been trying to decrypt.

She cross-referenced the login times with the library access records. J_Evans had signed in for three of those sessions.

This needed investigating.

The next morning, they woke and went to breakfast. It seemed as if everything was back to normal, that the events of the previous day hadn't happened. The refectory buzzed with noise: boys chatting, cutlery clattering.

Charlotte joined the queue for food. As she moved along the serving counter, she noticed a new face – a young woman with dark hair in a neat ponytail, wearing the standard catering uniform. She looked up as Charlotte approached and their eyes met.

Charlotte's breath caught in her throat. "Kaylee!"

Kaylee Smith smiled briefly, then composed herself. "Morning, Mrs Harper. What can I get you?"

"Scrambled eggs, please," Charlotte said, trying to keep her voice steady.

Kaylee served her a generous portion. "Heard you might need a hand," she said quietly. "Thought I'd return the favour. Helena and Grigore sent me."

Charlotte felt a rush of gratitude. A year ago, Kaylee had been homeless, sleeping in an abandoned building in Exmouth. Charlotte had helped her get back on her feet. She'd found her accommodation, helped her access benefits, and eventually secured her a job at a supermarket.

Kaylee had promised to repay her somehow.Charlotte had told her it wasn't necessary, but Kaylee had insisted. "If you ever need anything, call me. I mean it."

And now here she was.

"Thank you," Charlotte said quietly. "Really."

Kaylee gave her a slight nod and turned to serve the next person.

Angus was behind Charlotte in the queue. When he reached Kaylee his eyebrows rose slightly, but he kept his expression neutral. "Morning."

"Morning, Mr Harper. Full English?"

"Please."

They collected their food and found seats at the staff table. Angus leaned in, keeping his voice low. "I didn't know you'd contacted Kaylee."

"I didn't. Helena sent her. She offered to help. She's been looking for a way to help me."

Angus looked back at the serving counter. Kaylee was chatting easily with one of the other kitchen workers, already blending in. "She's doing well, then? Last I heard, she was at the supermarket."

"She's still there, I think. She must have taken time off to come here." Charlotte ate a forkful of her eggs. "Kitchen staff hear everything. If anyone's talking about what's going on – staff leaving, Oliver, whatever Brooke is up to – she'll hear."

Angus nodded. "We should brief her properly, let her know what we're looking for."

"Agreed. But not here. Too many ears to overhear. And it's better to speak in person rather than message, in case someone reads them on her phone."

They ate in silence for a few moments, both aware of the conversations around them. Boys were laughing too loudly, and the general chaos of a school morning surrounded them.

Charlotte spotted Kaylee again, clearing plates from one of the boys' tables. She was smiling, making small talk with them. She seemed natural, unassuming. She'd learned a lot in the last year. Getting back on her feet had given her confidence, and now she was using it to help them.

CHAPTER 14

Kaylee's first shift in the school kitchen had started at six in the morning. She'd been shown to a tiny room in the staff accommodation block the night before. It was barely big enough for a single bed and a chest of drawers, but it was warm and clean. After sleeping in an abandoned building last year, she wasn't about to complain. She was excited to be helping Charlotte and Angus, and had no doubts or hesitation when Helena had called her.

The kitchen was massive, industrial-sized, with stainless-steel surfaces and huge ovens. The smell of frying bacon filled the air. A woman in her fifties, wearing a hairnet and apron, looked up as Kaylee entered. A wave of anticipation went through her. She'd no experience in a kitchen, but she knew she was a quick learner, and if she kept her head down and worked hard, everything should be all right.

"You must be the new girl," she said. "Kaylee, is it?"

"That's right."

"I'm Donna, head cook. Been here fifteen years, so if you've got questions, ask me." She pointed to a younger man chopping vegetables at alarming speed. "That's Raj, our sous-chef. And over there is Karen."

Karen was older, maybe in her sixties, with grey hair and a kind smile. She was loading trays into a heated trolley. "Morning," she said, barely looking round.

"Right, then," Donna said. "Can you cook?"

"A bit."

"Good enough. You'll be helping prep breakfast, then serving at lunchtime. Dinner, too, if we're short-staffed. Karen will show you the ropes. Mostly, you'll be doing the skivvy jobs, like it says in the job description."

"Yeah, I know. I ain't afraid of hard work."

Karen gestured for Kaylee to follow her. "Come on, then. Bacon doesn't cook itself."

By mid-morning, Kaylee had already learned more than she'd expected. The kitchen staff talked constantly about the boys, the teachers, the school politics. It was better than any surveillance operation.

"They're good lads, mostly," Donna said, stirring a massive pot of soup. "But some of them are right terrors. The older ones, especially. They think they run the place."

"Which ones?" Kaylee asked, keeping her tone casual.

"The sixth-formers. Years 12 and 13. Some of them get special privileges. Lord knows why. Mr Brooke is always requesting cakes and biscuits. For chapel meetings, he calls them."

Kaylee's ears pricked up. "Chapel meetings?"

"Yeah. Every couple of weeks. Says it's academic enrichment, or some such nonsense. But he always wants the good stuff."

"Sounds expensive," Kaylee said.

"It is. But Brooke always gets what he wants. He's got the headmaster wrapped around his little finger." Donna lowered her voice. "Between you and me, I don't like him. I'm not sure what it is about him, but I just don't trust him."

Raj looked up from his chopping. "You're too suspicious, Donna."

"And you're too naïve, Raj."

Kaylee smiled and kept working. This was exactly the kind of information Charlotte and Angus would need.

At lunchtime, the refectory was chaos. Hundreds of boys lined up for food, shouting, jostling, laughing. Kaylee stood behind the serving counter with Karen, spooning pasta onto plates.

"Keep the portions even," Karen said. "Otherwise they'll complain. And don't let them have seconds until everyone's been served."

Kaylee nodded and got to work. The boys were polite enough, mostly. A few tried to charm her into giving them extra chips. She ignored them.

Then she noticed a boy near the back of the queue. He was thin, pale, with dark circles under his eyes. He picked up a tray but took only a bread roll and an apple.

"Is that all you want, love?" Kaylee asked.

The boy glanced at her, then away. "Not hungry."

"You sure? There's plenty."

"I'm fine." He moved on quickly.

Karen watched him go. "That's Kai. Headmaster wants us to keep an eye on what he's eating. Or rather, not eating."

"He looks terrible," Kaylee said.

"He does, poor lad. Apparently he just sits in his room, or wanders around like a ghost."

Kaylee made a mental note to keep an eye on him. She wondered what was making him so sad. Bullying? Homesickness? Something else?

Later that afternoon, Kaylee was wiping down tables in the refectory when Karen came over with a mop and bucket. "You settling in all right?" she asked.

"Yeah. Everyone's been really nice."

"Good. It's not a bad place to work, usually. Bit strange lately, though."

"Strange how?"

Karen leaned on her mop. "Didn't you see the story in the news?"

Kaylee shook her head.

Karen shrugged. "One of the boys tried to top himself. And before, other boys got hurt. Nothing major, but still. Broken wrist here, concussion there. Always excuses: fell down the stairs, tripped on the rugby pitch. Load of rubbish, if you ask me."

"You think someone's hurting them?"

Karen shrugged. "I don't know. But something's not right. And it's always the same group of boys: the ones who hang around with Mr Brooke."

Kaylee kept her expression neutral. "That sounds odd."

"Yeah. He runs some sort of club. Classical studies, or something posh like that. My friend worked here years ago, and there was a similar thing back then. Called themselves the Apollonian Society. Thought they were better than everyone else. It got shut down in the eighties after a boy got hurt."

"What happened?"

"I don't know the details. But it was bad enough that the headmaster at the time banned it. Thought it was gone for good." Karen straightened up. "But if you ask me, it's back. Or something like it is."

Kaylee absorbed this. She needed to text this info to Charlotte and Angus.

CHAPTER 15

Charlotte was heading back to the flat after her afternoon lessons when she saw the matron, Mrs Hodge, leaving the medical rooms.

Charlotte paused. "Hello."

Mrs Hodge stopped and smiled at her. "Everything all right, Mrs Harper? Settling in okay?"

"Yes, fine. I just wanted to ask you something. About the boys."

Mrs Hodge's expression didn't change, but she gestured to the medical-room door. "Come in, then. Better to talk in private."

Charlotte followed her inside. The room was small but well organised. A bed with clean white sheets, a desk cluttered with forms, cabinets stocked with bandages and medicines. It smelt of antiseptic.

Mrs Hodge closed the door and leaned against her desk. "What do you want to know?"

"I've noticed that some of the boys seem a bit on edge. Nervous. I wondered if you'd noticed it too."

"I have. But after what happened with Oliver, it's no surprise."

"Has anything like this happened before? Boys getting hurt, I mean. Or acting strangely."

Mrs Hodge was quiet for a moment, studying Charlotte's face. Then she sighed. "You're not just asking out of curiosity, are you?"

Charlotte met her eyes. "I'm concerned, that's all."

Mrs Hodge folded her arms. "Well, since you're asking, yes. There was a boy last term. Year 10. He came to me with a broken wrist and concussion. Said he'd fallen down the back stairs behind the science block."

"You didn't believe him?"

"Not for a second. The injuries didn't match the story. And the way he looked at me when I asked what had happened." She shuddered. "He was terrified. He'd clearly been threatened with something if he told anyone what had really happened."

"What did you do?"

"I reported it to the headmaster, and told him I thought the boy had been pushed or attacked. But without the boy confirming it, there was nothing anyone could do."

"And the boy?"

"He left at the end of term. His parents pulled him out and sent him to a boarding school in Canada, if you can believe it. No goodbye, no notice. Just gone."

"Did the parents say why?"

Mrs Hodge shook her head. "They wouldn't talk about it, but I could tell they were spooked. Really spooked. They wanted to get their son as far away from this place as possible."

"Do you think it's connected to what happened to Oliver?"

"I don't know. Maybe. This place has layers. Some are beautiful: the history, the tradition, the education. But some of them…"

Charlotte stared at Mrs Hodge, who straightened up. "I've already said more than I should. Just watch yourself, and that husband of yours. Don't trust everything you hear. And don't assume that the people in charge have your best interests at heart."

Before Charlotte could respond, the door opened and a boy stumbled in, clutching his stomach. "Miss, I don't feel well," he mumbled.

Mrs Hodge immediately shifted into matron mode. "Right, sit down and let me have a look at you." She glanced at Charlotte, who took the hint and left.

As she walked down the corridor, her mind was spinning. A boy last term, hurt, terrified, and sent to Canada. And now Oliver in hospital. It wasn't a coincidence. It couldn't be.

She hurried to the staff accommodation, wondering whether Mrs Hodge was warning her out of kindness or malice. But when she reached the door to their flat, she stopped dead.

A yellow Post-it note was stuck to the door. On it was written in block capitals: QUIT NOW.

Charlotte looked up and down the corridor. Whoever had left the note was long gone.

She pulled the note off the door and stared at it. Neat, printed letters. Anonymous. Untraceable.

Did someone know about them? Surely not. How could they know?

She unlocked the door and entered the flat, her hands shaking slightly. She bolted the door behind her and checked the cameras outside the door. She rewound the footage.

There. Twenty minutes ago. A figure in a dark hoodie, face in shadow, walked up to the door, stuck the note on and walked away. No hesitation, no looking around. Just calm, deliberate action.

Charlotte couldn't see the person's face. Couldn't tell if it was a student or a member of staff. But the message was clear. They were being watched.

She pulled out her phone and called Angus. He answered on the second ring. "Hey, everything okay?"

"No. Someone left a note on our door. '*Quit now,*' it says."

There was a pause. "What?"

"A Post-it note. Someone put it there while we were out. I've got it on camera, but I can't see their face."

"I'm coming back now. Don't leave the flat."

"I won't."

"Charlotte, I mean it. Lock the door. Don't open it for anyone except me."

"I've already locked it."

"Good. I'll be there in five minutes."

Charlotte hung up and sat on the edge of the bed, staring at the Post-it note in her hand.

Angus arrived four minutes later and took the Post-it note from Charlotte's hand. "Quit now," he read aloud.

He looked at her. "Have you shown the footage to anyone?"

"Not yet."

"Let me see it."

Charlotte pulled up the camera feed on her laptop. They watched the hooded figure approach, stick the note on the door and leave. The whole thing took less than ten seconds.

"Can you enhance it?" Angus asked.

"I can try, but I don't think it'll help. They covered their face. It could be any one of the students or several members of staff."

Angus replayed the footage. "From the height and build, looks as if it could be a student. Or a small adult. Can't tell the gender, either, although the odds are in favour of a male."

"They look as if they knew what they were doing," Charlotte said. "This wasn't some kid playing a prank. This was deliberate."

Angus sat down beside her. "We need to be more careful. If they're leaving notes, they're watching us. They might know we're not just teachers. We need to proceed along those lines."

"Do you think Freddie might have told someone?"

Angus frowned. "Why would he? He brought us in to go undercover. He'd be undermining himself."

Charlotte thought over the last few days. She'd asked questions, looked into records, talked to Kaylee, checked the encrypted drive. Any one of those things could have tipped someone off.

"What do we do?" she asked.

Angus was quiet for a moment. "We keep going," he said, eventually. "But we'll be more careful. No more asking direct questions. No more snooping in places we shouldn't be. We blend in and watch, and Kaylee does the same."

"What if things escalate?"

"Then we get out. For now, we stay. Because whatever's going on here is bad enough that someone's willing to threaten us."

Charlotte looked at the Post-it note again.

Quit now.

"Not a chance," she whispered to herself.

CHAPTER 16

Charlotte couldn't sleep: her mind wouldn't switch off. She lay in the darkness, listening to Angus's steady breathing beside her, and eventually gave up.

She slipped out of bed, grabbed her laptop, and moved to the desk in the corner. The flat was cold. She pulled a blanket around her shoulders and opened the laptop, the screen's glow harsh in the dark room.

She'd been working on the encrypted drive for days now, but it was proving harder to crack than she'd expected. Whoever had set it up knew what they were doing. It would take time.

But there were other things she could look at: patterns in the school's network that might tell her something.

She pulled up the server logs again. She'd been through them before, but only briefly. Now she had time to dig deeper.

She started with the admin accounts. There were three: the headmaster, the deputy head, Miss James, and the IT administrator, someone called J. Evans. She'd never met Evans, hadn't even seen them around the school. They probably worked remotely or only came in occasionally. She'd ask Freddie next time she saw him.

Charlotte filtered the logs to show only admin activity over the past month.

Most of it was routine. Freddie logging in during office hours. Miss James accessing files in the evenings, probably doing marking or admin work. Evans appearing sporadically, usually during the day.

But then something caught her eye. Late-night logins, from the admin account belonging to J. Evans.

Charlotte frowned and clicked through the entries.

October 15th - 11:37pm - Admin_JEvans - Library Terminal03

October 18th - 12:03am - Admin_JEvans - MusicRoom01

October 22nd - 11:45pm - Admin_JEvans - Library Terminal03

October 25th - 12:15am - Admin_JEvans - MusicRoom01

Charlotte sat back. Why would a remote IT administrator be logging in from student terminals in the middle of the night? And why always in the library or the music room?

She cross-referenced the times with the building access logs. The library was supposed to be locked by 9 p.m. The music department was closed after 8 p.m. So whoever was using those terminals had a key – or knew how to get in without one.

She dug deeper. What had they been accessing?

The logs showed file activity. Admin_JEvans had been opening files on the encrypted drive. The one Charlotte had been trying to crack.

She filtered the network traffic logs and found something else.

Encrypted messages. Dozens of them, all sent from the school's server to an external IP address.

Charlotte ran the IP through a lookup tool, and her stomach turned over.

The messages were going to a server in Russia.

She copied the IP address, the timestamps, the file names. Everything. Then she saved it all to a USB drive and ejected it.

This wasn't just about a secret society or a manipulative teacher. This was something else. Something bigger.

Charlotte closed the laptop and sat in the darkness, her mind racing. She looked at Angus, still fast asleep. She wouldn't wake him. It could wait until morning.

The next morning, Charlotte told Angus what she'd found. "We need to ask Freddie who J Evans is," she said, once she'd explained everything. "They're meant to be an IT administrator, but I've never seen them. And I doubt they're supposed to be logging in at midnight from student computers."

"Could it be someone using their account?"

"Maybe. But they'd need the password, and admin passwords are supposed to be secure."

"Or Evans is involved, and using student computers to cover their tracks."

"But wouldn't they either use a student's ID or create a 'student ID', rather than use their own?"

Charlotte pondered. "Perhaps."

"What about the messages to Russia?"

"I don't know. They could be anything. Data theft, espionage, fraud. But it's serious. Schools don't have encrypted hard disks on their devices."

Angus was quiet for a moment, thinking. "Do we tell Freddie?"

Charlotte frowned. "I don't know. I suppose that if Evans is involved and Freddie doesn't know, we can tell him, and then he can deal with it."

Angus rubbed his face. "What about someone else? Miss James? She knows who we really are."

Charlotte considered. "Maybe. But she's the deputy head. If something dodgy is happening with the IT systems, she should already know. And if she doesn't, that's either incompetence or wilful ignorance."

"Or she's being kept in the dark too."

"This is most likely to be the case."

"I think we keep investigating on our own," Charlotte said, eventually. "For now, at least. We don't know who to trust. The only people we can be sure of are each other, Freddie, and Kaylee."

Angus nodded slowly. "Agreed. But we need to be even more careful. If this is connected to Russia, we're not just dealing with a dodgy teacher any more. This could be organised crime. Or worse."

"I know."

"And if they're willing to leave threatening notes, they're willing to do more than that. I wonder if any of the students are Russian. Do we have access to the student info?"

Charlotte smiled and began tapping at the keyboard. "Not officially, but..."

"You've hacked into the server and you can get all the details you need?"

"You know me so well."

Charlotte set about looking through the boys' details. "Looks like there's two Russian pupils: Artem Petrov and Matvey Volkov. One is in year 10; the other is in year 11."

"We'll need to keep on eye on them."

"How, though? We can't exactly spy on them. This is a school, and they're children."

"Through the lessons, obviously. We could get Kaylee to keep an eye on them too."

Charlotte pulled up the logs again. "I need to find out who J. Evans really is. Check staff records, payroll, anything. And I want to see if I can trace those messages to Russia. Find out what's being sent, and why."

"I'll keep an eye on the students," said Angus. "See if anyone's sneaking into the library or music room late at night. Maybe I'll stake it out one evening."

Charlotte gave a dismissive wave of her hand. "No need. I'll put software on the two computers being used, which makes them record who's using them. It switches on the camera."

She downloaded the files on to her USB drive and put it in her pocket. "This stays with me. If anything happens, this is evidence."

Angus's eyebrows shot up. "If anything happens to *you*? We're not putting you in danger."

"You know what I mean." Charlotte closed the laptop and stood up. "Come on. We've got breakfast, then lessons. Let's try to act like normal teachers for a few hours."

"Of course. Normal teachers who've just uncovered a potential international crime ring operating out of a private school."

Charlotte smiled grimly. "Exactly."

They left the flat together, locking the door behind them. But as they walked down the corridor, Charlotte couldn't shake the feeling that they were being watched.

The Post-it note had been a warning. And now they'd found something even bigger.

CHAPTER 17

Charlotte found Freddie in his office during morning break. He was hunched over his desk, surrounded by paperwork, looking more exhausted than she'd ever seen him.

"Got a minute?" she asked, knocking on the open door.

He looked up and waved her in. "Of course. Close the door."

Charlotte shut the door and sat in one of the chairs facing his desk. The surface was cluttered with folders, papers, and what looked like budget spreadsheets. A framed photo of Freddie in running gear at a race finish line on the wall. Behind him, the bookshelves were packed with books on safeguarding, leadership, and education.

"I wanted to ask you something," she began. "The IT administrator, J. Evans. Who is it?"

Freddie leaned back in his chair. "Jeremy Evans? He's a contractor, comes in once a month to sort out IT issues. Why?"

"I'm just trying to get to know who's who. I haven't met him yet."

"You probably won't: he mostly works remotely. Fixes things from his office, and apart from his scheduled monthly visit he only comes in if there's a major problem. He was awarded the contract before I became head, so I've just kept it going. The rate's good, and the trustees are happy with the service, as am I."

Charlotte nodded. "How long has he been working for the school?"

"About five years, I think. Maybe six. He's very reliable. We had a major server crash last year. Everything went down and we lost access to all our files. Evans fixed it remotely within a few hours. He saved us thousands in data recovery costs."

"That's impressive."

"It is. And the best part is, he runs a CIC. A nonprofit Community Interest Company. He employs disabled people, helps them get into IT work. Very admirable. He even got an OBE in the honours list a couple of years ago."

Charlotte felt a flicker of doubt. An OBE was significant. You didn't receive an honour from the king for no reason.

"So he's legitimate, then," she said, trying not to let her disappointment show.

"Very. I've had no complaints. The systems run smoothly, and when there's a problem, he sorts it quickly. Why? Is there an issue with the computers in your classroom?"

"No, everything's fine. I was just curious." She didn't want to tell him everything because despite the fact he was paying them for this, they didn't want him rushing in, or acting differently towards people.

Freddie studied her, his tired eyes sharp. "Is this about the investigation?"

"Everything is about the investigation. I've been looking through the network logs. Just routine stuff, trying to get a sense of how things work. Evans's name came up a few times, that's all."

"And?"

"And nothing. I wanted to know who he was before I dug any deeper, just to check. Everyone needs looking at."

Freddie rubbed his face. "Look, if you think Evans is involved in something, I need to know. The trustees will have my head if there's been any kind of security breach."

"I'm not saying he's involved. I'm just being thorough."

"All right. But keep me posted, eh? The last thing this school needs is another scandal."

"I will."

Charlotte stood up to leave, then paused. "This server crash last year ... when did it happen?"

Freddie thought. "October, I think. Around the middle of the month. Not quite half-term. Why?"

"Just wondered. By the way, there's a load of old telecoms and electronics in the skip. Mind if I take it for an afterschool electronics club?"

Freddie looked intrigued and shrugged. "Sure. Just make sure you fill out a risk-assessment form. Don't want any boys electrocuted." He gave a small laugh.

Charlotte groaned inwardly. Risk assessment? It was electrical equipment. One of the best things about playing around with it was the occasional electric shock. "Of course," she said with a smile. "And don't worry, I'll make sure the boys aren't harmed."

"When are you thinking of running it?"

"ASAP. Assuming we're going to get to the bottom of this mystery quickly. Tomorrow?"

"Sounds perfect. I'm sure some of the boys would love to learn some electronics."

"Thanks, Freddie. See you later."

She left his office and headed back to the flat. Angus was there, marking worksheets from his GCSE PE classes. "Well?" he asked, looking up.

"Evans is a contractor. CIC company, employs disabled people, got an OBE for it. Freddie says he's legitimate."

"An OBE?"

"Yeah. Which makes me think that maybe we're barking up the wrong tree. You don't get an honour for running a dodgy IT operation."

"Or it's very good cover," Angus replied.

"I'm not sure. The late-night logins are still suspicious, though. And the messages to Russia. I haven't told Freddie any of this, not yet. It could be that someone has got Evans's password and is using it."

"What do you want to do?"

Charlotte thought. "I want to check him out properly. Not just the network logs – his company, his background, everything. And I want someone to go to his office and see what's actually there."

"Grigore?"

"Yes."

Angus nodded. "All right. But if Evans is legitimate and we're wrong, we may end up looking like paranoid idiots."

"Better to be a paranoid idiot than miss something important."

Later that day, Grigore texted Charlotte: *At the office. Looks legit. Will call later.*

That evening, Charlotte put him on speakerphone so Angus could listen too.

"What did you find?" Charlotte asked.

"Small office in Matford Industrial Estate," Grigore said, his voice tinny through the phone. "Ground floor, professional building. Sign outside say 'Evans IT Solutions CIC.' Looks legitimate. I vent in, said I vas looking for IT services for my business. Receptionist very polite, gave me brochure."

"What was inside?"

"Offices. One for Evans, open plan mainly, one is workspace for staff. I saw two people working, both in wheelchairs. They were doing genuine IT work. Monitors, coding, fixing computers. Not fake."

"Did you see Evans?"

"No. But I saw photo on wall of him receiving OBE at Buckingham Palace. Looks real. I took photos, will send you."

Charlotte felt her certainty wavering. "Anything suspicious?"

"Not really. Office is clean, organised. Certificates on wall, testimonials from clients. They do IT work for schools, charities, small businesses. Everything checks out."

"Nothing that suggests anything dodgy?"

Grigore was quiet for a moment. "I cannot say for sure. But if this is front, it very good front. Very convincing."

Charlotte sighed. "All right. Thanks, Grigore."

"You vant me to keep vatching?"

"I want you to hack into their network."

"Of course."

CHAPTER 18

After the update from Grigore, Charlotte decided to visit the server room and look at the machine that was sending messages to Russia.

"End of the science corridor, ground floor," Freddie had said, when she'd asked where it was. "Though I'm not sure you'll find much of use in there. It's just a computer in a room."

Charlotte hadn't responded to that comment. The server might be "just a computer in a room" to Freddie, but to her, it needed checking out.

"Have you got a key? I assume the room is locked?"

Freddie rummaged in his desk and pulled out a cash box. Inside was an assortment of different keys. "I'm sure it's here somewhere."

He checked each label until he'd been through them all. "Hmm. Not sure where my key is. I'll check with Evans when he's next in. He probably forgot to return it."

Charlotte smiled and nodded. A locked door wouldn't stop her going in.

A few minutes later, Charlotte stood in front of a plain

wooden door at the end of a long corridor. The door had a Yale lock.

She glanced up and down the corridor, then pulled out her lockpick set and got to work on the mechanism. Twenty seconds later, the lock clicked. She opened the door and stepped inside, closing it behind her.

The room was smaller than she'd expected. It could fit in a maximum of three people. There were no windows, and a single bare bulb dangled from the ceiling. The walls were lined with metal shelving units, stacked with boxes of old paperwork and dusty textbooks from decades ago. It looked more like a storage cupboard than a server room, except at the far end, against the back wall, was a server rack.

Charlotte moved through the clutter, stepping over boxes, and approached the rack. She'd expected something to match the building, and specifically the room. Old, outdated, probably running Windows Server 2003 or something equally ancient, but the rack was modern. Suspiciously modern. It must be only a year or two old, and it stuck out like a sore thumb in its contrast to the rest of the room.

Charlotte examined it. It was an expensive piece of kit, the sort of thing more often seen in new data centres than an old private school in the middle of Devon.

She crouched to examine it more closely, then pulled out her phone and took a few photos. The server's model number, the network switches, the cabling.

Then she noticed something else. A second machine was tucked below the main server. It was smaller, but equally modern. It had no branding, just a plain black case, with a single Ethernet cable running from it to the network switch.

What's this for?

Judging by the blinking lights, the machine was definitely doing something.

She looked for a way to access it, but there was no monitor, no keyboard, no way to see what it was running. Just the black case and the network connection.

A hidden server on the school network. Unbranded, and unaccounted for.

Charlotte took more photos, then stood up and looked around the room again. The clutter of old paperwork and broken equipment was perfect camouflage. Anyone who glanced in would think this was just a storage room. They'd never look closely enough to see the expensive hardware hidden at the back.

She took a last look around to check she hadn't missed anything, then slipped out and closed the door, checking it was locked.

Someone had gone to a lot of trouble to make sure the server room looked unimportant. That meant whatever was on those machines was very important indeed, and somehow, she had to access it.

CHAPTER 19

Grigore parked Charlotte's Volvo across the street from Evans IT Solutions and switched off the engine. The office was exactly as he'd described to Charlotte the day before. Ground floor, a professional building with clean signage. Through the window, he could see the reception area. The same woman sat at the desk, typing.

He glanced at his watch: 9:15 a.m. The office had been open for fifteen minutes.

Grigore reached for the laptop bag on the passenger seat and pulled out the small Wi-Fi adapter Charlotte had given him. He plugged it into his laptop and ran the software she'd installed. Now it would attempt to connect to the office's wireless network.

He'd done this before: Charlotte had taught him how. Find the network, run the script, wait for it to crack the password. Usually it took about twenty minutes, though sometimes longer if the password was complex.

A black window appeared on the laptop's screen, with lines of green text scrolling rapidly.

The software scanned for networks. Three appeared on the screen.

Evans_IT_Staff

CaffeBest_Public

Evans_IT_Guest

Grigore selected *Evans_IT_Guest* first. Guest Wi-Fi might be easier to crack.

The software got to work. Lines of text scrolled by. Grigore watched the progress bar inch forward.

Ten minutes passed, then twenty.

The scrolling stopped and a message flashed up on the screen: *Password encryption too strong. Unable to crack.*

Grigore frowned. Then he opened the advanced program which Charlotte had told him to try if the first one didn't work.

This one took longer, but an hour later, he had the same result. The encryption was too good. Military grade, Charlotte would say. No surprise for an IT company, but frustrating nonetheless.

He texted Charlotte: *Cannot get into Wi-Fi. Too secure.*

Her reply came a minute later: *OK, go to phase 2. Use the laptop.*

Grigore looked at the laptop bag on the seat beside him. Inside was the old Toshiba which Charlotte had prepared. He picked up his phone and checked the Evans IT Solutions website. A banner on the homepage said *Free Weekly Computer Clinic – Wednesdays, 10am-12pm. Bring your broken laptop and we'll fix it for free.*

He checked the date. Today was Wednesday.

He glanced at his watch again. Ten thirty-five.

Grigore locked the car and walked down the street to a small café. He ordered a black coffee and sat by the window, watching the office across the road. A few people came and went. A delivery driver dropped off a package. A man in a suit entered and left ten minutes later, carrying a laptop bag. None of it looked overtly suspicious.

At 9:55, Grigore finished his coffee, picked up the laptop bag, and crossed the street.

The reception area was exactly as he remembered: clean, tidy, professional-looking. The receptionist, in her mid-forties, with dark hair and a kind face, looked up and smiled as he entered. "Hello, again. How can I help you?"

Grigore held up the laptop bag. "Free computer clinic today? I bring my laptop. It broken."

"Of course! Just take this ticket and have a seat in the lounge area over there. Someone will be with you as soon as possible."

Grigore took the ticket, which had the number four on it.

Half an hour later, it was finally Grigore's turn. Two people were running the clinic, but those seeking help before him seemed to take forever.

"Number four?" a man in a shabby T-shirt and jeans said. He was thin and about forty years old.

Grigore stood up and followed the man to one of the nearby desks.

"I'm Mark," the man said. "You've got a broken laptop?"

"Yez." Grigore set the bag on the desk and pulled out the Toshiba. "It does not start. Just blue screen with error."

Mark took the laptop, opened it and pressed the power button. The screen lit up, displayed the manufacturer's logo, then switched to a blue screen with white text: *CRITICAL_SYSTEM_ERROR. Your PC ran into a problem and needs to restart.*

"Ah, yeah. Classic," Mark said. "Looks like a corrupted OS. Happens sometimes with older machines. When did this start?"

"Yesterday. It was working, then it just stopped."

"All right, let's have a look. This shouldn't take long. We'll try a system repair first. If that doesn't work, we might need to reinstall Windows, but I'll back up your files first if we go down that route."

"Zank you."

Grigore watched as Mark worked on the laptop. Twenty minutes passed as Mark pressed buttons, restarted the laptop several times, and plugged in a USB flash drive. Eventually, the familiar Windows music started and the laptop sprang into life.

"All sorted," Mark said, closing the laptop and handing it to him. "As I thought, it was a corrupted system file. I ran a repair tool and fixed it. Should be good as new now."

"Zank you. How much I owe?"

Mark smiled. "It's free. That's the whole point of the clinic."

"You are very kind."

"No problem. If it happens again, just bring it back."

Grigore took the laptop, thanked him again and left.

Back in the car, he opened the laptop and checked it. It booted up normally now, with no blue screen.

He texted Charlotte: *Done. Laptop fixed. But he plug in USB, should I be worried?*

Her reply: *That's great. Shut the laptop down. Don't turn it back on until I can check that he hasn't put anything dodgy on it with that USB.*

Grigore shut down the laptop and put it back in the bag. Then he started the car's engine, pulled out of the parking space and drove away.

Phase two complete. Now Charlotte's virus would be working its way through the Evans IT network.

CHAPTER 20

At seven o'clock that evening, Charlotte and Angus were back in their quarters at the school. Charlotte pulled out her laptop and connected it remotely to her home network.

"This'll take a minute," she told Angus, who was sitting beside her. "I need to check if the payload deployed."

Angus raised his eyebrows. "What exactly is a payload?"

Charlotte didn't look up. "Just the virus."

She opened a terminal window and lines of code scrolled past.

"Good," she murmured. "It's active."

"So it worked?"

"Yep. My secret virus is now installed on their network. Every time someone in that office sends an email, accesses a file, or logs into a server, the virus will record it and send me the data. I'll be able to see everything they're doing."

"And they won't know?"

"Not unless they're very good. Even then, I've hidden it well. It'll take weeks for them to find it. And if they do, it just deletes itself."

Angus watched the code scrolling for a few moments. "What now?"

"Now, we wait. The virus will take a few hours to start sending data. By tonight, I should have access to their entire network."

"And then?"

"Then I'll know if Evans is innocent or not. If he's involved in something, eventually it'll show up in his emails, his files, his server activity. If we don't see anything that incriminates Evans, then someone else is using his username and password."

Later that evening, Charlotte was sitting at the little desk, staring at the screen. Data had started coming in. Emails, file transfers, login records. Everything that happened on the Evans IT network was now visible to her.

She scrolled through the emails first. Most of them were mundane. Quotes for clients, support tickets, invoices. Mark, the man who'd fixed Grigore's laptop, was corresponding with a school in Plymouth about a server upgrade. Another staff member was helping a charity set up a new database. It all looked legitimate.

Charlotte moved on to the file server, where she found client files, project documents, and financial records. She opened a few at random. They all matched what she would expect from a small IT company.

Angus was standing by the window, looking out and thinking about the case, when he glimpsed two figures walking alongside the building. Their hoods were up and they were moving fast, keeping close to the wall and staying in the shadows.

He squinted, trying to make out who they were, but the light was too dim. The figures moved with purpose, glancing around every so often as if to check they weren't being watched.

"Two people are acting suspiciously outside," Angus said. "I'm going to head out and investigate."

Charlotte, still gazing at the screen, didn't respond.

Angus sighed, then grabbed his coat and slipped outside. The evening air felt cool on his face.

He kept to the edge of the path, following the route the two figures had taken, keeping out of sight even though they'd had a head start. Something told him this wasn't normal. Boys didn't sneak around school grounds at night unless they were up to something.

He turned the corner. In front of him was the old music block, where Charlotte had mentioned that Admin_JEvans had logged in from a computer multiple times, late at night.

Angus moved closer to the music block, keeping to the shadows. The building was old, made of stone, with tall, arched windows. A side door stood slightly ajar but was closing. He crept towards it, but by the time he reached it, the door had shut.

He moved along the wall to one of the windows. A faint light glowed within. He crouched and peered through the glass at the bottom.

Six or seven boys were sitting in a circle on the floor. They were talking, their faces serious. One of them, older, maybe a year 12 pupil, seemed to be leading the discussion. The others listened intently.

Angus strained to hear, but the window was too thick. He could see their mouths moving but couldn't make out the words.

Then a hand touched his shoulder. Angus spun round, heart hammering.

Charlotte was standing behind him.

"Jesus Christ!" Angus muttered, moving her away from the window. "I just lost ten years of my life."

"Sorry," Charlotte whispered, not looking particularly

sorry. "You just got up and left, and I wondered what you were doing."

"I told you, not that you were listening. I saw two people sneaking about outside our window, so I followed them. They're in there. Six or seven pupils, sitting in a circle, talking."

Charlotte moved to the window and peered in. "Maybe they're just ... talking?"

Angus gave her a look.

"All right, all right. I agree that no one's out at this time of night in a semi-secret location for a good reason."

"There's a computer in this room, isn't there?"

Charlotte pressed her face closer to the glass. "Yes, but they're nowhere near it."

"What do we do? Go in, or report them to Freddie?"

Charlotte thought for a moment. "Neither. In the morning, I'll break into the music department and plant some bugs. Then we can find out exactly what they're up to."

Angus peeped through the window. The boys were still talking, animated now. One gestured emphatically. Another shook his head.

"Come on," Charlotte whispered. "Let's go, before they spot us."

They moved away, keeping low, and headed back to their flat. Once inside, Angus locked the door, and Charlotte sat down at the desk.

"A secret meeting in the music block," she said. "The same place where Evans's account was accessing the network."

"You think it's connected?"

"Has to be. It's too much of a coincidence."

Angus took off his coat and hung it up. "So what are they doing in there? Was that a meeting of the secret society?"

"Maybe," said Charlotte. "Or it could be something completely different. We'll know once I get those bugs in place."

CHAPTER 21

The next morning, Charlotte waited until the school was busy. Lessons were in full swing, corridors empty. She picked up a small bag, slipped out of the flat, and headed for the music block.

The door was locked, but she'd anticipated that. She pulled out her set of lockpicks. Thirty seconds later, the door clicked open.

She stepped inside and closed it behind her.

The room was dusty, unused. Old music stands leaned against the walls. A piano sat in the corner, covered with a sheet. The floor was marked with flecks of mud and footprints where the boys had been sitting the night before. She wondered whether the new music room was better. Maybe she'd visit it later.

Charlotte took two small devices from her bag. Audio bugs, each no bigger than a coin. She placed one behind a radiator, and another on the underside of a music stand.

Then she checked her phone. The bugs were active, transmitting to her laptop back in the flat. Job done.

She inched the door open, checked that the coast was

clear, then slipped out, and locked the door behind her. Time to head to her classroom.

Charlotte's lessons in the morning were tiring, but enjoyable. She was starting to get into teaching programming. At lunchtime, after eating, she went over to some of the students she'd taught the day before, and offered them house points in return for their help with removing the electrical equipment from the skip and into the computer room.

She laid everything out on the desks at the back of the room: the telephones, the headphones with their curly cords, the language lab tape recorders, the amplifier, the multimeters from the physics department, and the stack of circuit boards from the old intercom system. It looked like a museum display. Or a car boot sale. She wasn't sure which.

Angus appeared in the doorway, still in his PE kit. "What on earth are you doing?"

"Setting up for the electronics club. After school. I told you, didn't I?"

"No, you must have forgotten. This looks like you've raided a Cold War bunker."

"It's just a few old bits and pieces from the skip. There's gold in here, if you know where to look."

Angus picked up one of the dial telephones and turned it over in his hands. "We had one just like this, growing up." He put it to his ear and listened to nothing, then smiled. "I miss these, actually. There was something satisfying about dialling a number properly. The weight of the handset, the click of the dial going round, the little whirr as it returned. You felt like you were doing something. Now you just prod a screen and it's all over in a second."

"You sound about ninety," Charlotte said.

"I'm serious. Everything's too easy now. No one has to

remember a phone number any more. I can still remember our phone number, growing up."

Charlotte took the telephone from him and held it up. "Well, I'll tell you what. I'm going to see if any of the boys know how to use a finger dial. I bet you none of them do. And if any of them can work it out without being shown, they'll get a heap of house points."

"Do you remember when your phreaking got us out of that mess on Dartmoor?"

Charlotte nodded. "Hard to forget. Maybe one day, it will help some of these boys."

"I didn't even know what phreaking was before that."

"Most people don't. That's the point." Charlotte smiled at the memory. "It's a dying art. Almost no one alive knows how the old telephone exchanges really worked. But the principles behind it are still relevant. More relevant than ever, actually. It's just that nobody teaches it."

"Until now."

"Until now."

Angus put the telephone down. "And the boys are keen on this, are they?"

"I've got six signed up. One of them asked if they'd be building a bomb."

"Please tell me you said no."

"I said not this week." Charlotte grinned at his face. "I'm joking. Obviously I said no."

"Well, have fun." Angus kissed Charlotte on the cheek and left.

At four o'clock, eight boys filed into the computer suite. Daniel Brooke was first, as Charlotte had expected, his own laptop already tucked under his arm. Behind him came a mix of year groups: two year 7s who looked slightly terrified, three year 9s trying to look as if they didn't care, and a tall year 11 boy Charlotte didn't recognise.

"Right, everyone, grab a stool and sit at the back where the equipment is. Don't touch anything yet."

The boys arranged themselves around the desks. A few of them eyed the old telephones with curiosity. One of the year 7s poked the PA amplifier and jumped back when it rocked on the desk.

"Welcome to Electronics Club," Charlotte said. "I'm Mrs Harper, and I'm going to teach you something that most adults don't know and most teachers wouldn't dream of showing you."

She held up one of the dial telephones. "But first, a challenge. Does anyone in this room know how to use one of these? Ten house points for Coleridge if you can work it out without being shown."

The boys stared at the telephone. One of the year 9s put his finger on the number five and pushed it. Nothing happened.

"You turn it," another boy said. He tried anti-clockwise. It barely moved.

"Other way," Charlotte said.

He pulled it round until his finger hit the metal stop. When he let go, the dial whirred back to its resting position.

"That's it! Ten points for your house."

The boy looked stunned. "Ten points? Just for using a phone?"

"For working out how to use a piece of technology you've never seen before. That's problem-solving. That's what this club is about."

She held the telephone up again. "Now, the real stuff. Back in the sixties and seventies, the telephone network was controlled by audio tones. If you knew the right frequencies, you could do things with the phone system that the phone companies didn't want you to do. People who figured this out were called phreakers. Phone freaks. And some of them went on to change the world. Steve Wozniak and Steve Jobs built devices called blue boxes before they ever built Apple. Wozniak once used one to phone the Vatican and pretend to be Henry Kissinger."

"No way," Daniel said. "Who's Henry Kissinger?"

"A sort of American politician. The point is, phreaking was the grandfather of hacking. And today, you're going to take these telephones apart, salvage the components, and build a simple tone generator. Right. Everyone take a telephone and a screwdriver."

For the next hour, the room was a mess of dismantled handsets, salvaged circuit boards, and boys hunched over breadboards with multimeters. Charlotte moved between them, helping, correcting, showing them how to read resistor colour codes and test components. Daniel was the first to get his circuit working. A thin, reedy tone came from the telephone earpiece he'd connected as a speaker.

One by one, the other boys got their circuits working. The room filled with overlapping tones of different pitches, a dissonant choir of electronic squeals.

"This is what a dying robot sounds like," one of the year 9s said, adjusting his resistor rapidly.

"Miss, mine's really low," the year 7 boy said. His circuit was producing a deep, slow pulse, more of a click than a tone.

"That's because your capacitor is too large. Swap it for a smaller one." Charlotte handed him a tiny capacitor. He swapped it, and the tone leaped up to a high-pitched whine. The boy's face lit up.

Charlotte looked at the clock. Five fifteen. "Right, everyone, we need to wrap up. But before you go—"

She took Daniel's circuit and connected it to the broken PA amplifier she'd rescued from the skip. She'd spent ten minutes at lunch replacing a blown fuse inside it. She switched it on, and Daniel's thin tone became a room-filling buzz that rattled the windows.

The boys covered their ears, laughing.

Charlotte turned the volume down. "That's amplification. Next week, we're taking the tape recorders apart and building a radio receiver. Look up crystal radio sets tonight. They don't even need a battery."

The boys packed up, chatting excitedly. Daniel lingered.

"Miss, this is amazing. I've never done anything like this before."

"There's a whole world of electronics that most people never see," Charlotte said, tidying the components into boxes. "Someone had to build the first circuits, the first computers, the first phones. And they did it with components just like these."

Daniel smiled. "Thanks, miss. See you next week."

He left, and Charlotte stood alone in the room, surrounded by dismantled telephones and salvaged circuit boards. She felt something she hadn't expected. Pride.

She packed up and switched off the lights. As she locked the door, Angus appeared at the end of the corridor.

"How did it go?"

"Brilliantly. They loved it."

"So, basically, you taught a group of teenage boys how to make annoying high-pitched noises from school equipment?"

Charlotte linked her arm through his as they walked towards the flat. "Yes. And next week, we're building a radio."

"God help us all."

Charlotte laughed. For a moment, she forgot about Evans, the encrypted server, the threatening notes, and the frightened boys meeting in secret in the music block. For a moment, she was just a teacher who'd had a good day.

CHAPTER 22

Later that day, Charlotte was alone in the staffroom when Kaylee came in. "Got a minute?" she asked.

Charlotte looked up. "Of course. How's it going?"

Kaylee sat down and filled her in on Donna's comments about Brooke and the chapel meetings, Karen's mention of the Apollonian Society, and Kai barely eating.

Charlotte listened, her expression growing more serious. "The Apollonian Society," she said. "That's new."

"Karen said it was shut down in the eighties. But she thinks it's back."

"And Brooke is running it?"

"Looks like it."

Charlotte tapped her pen against her leg. "This is good work, Kaylee. Really good. Angus and I spotted some boys having a meeting in the old music room last night. I wonder if that could be the Apollonian Society."

Kaylee shrugged. "Could be. How many boys were there?"

"Six or seven. They all looked quite senior: like sixth-formers, or possibly slightly younger." Then she put down her pen and studied Kaylee. "What's it like, working in the kitchen? I'm guessing it's not exactly glamorous."

Kaylee smiled. "It's fine. Donna and the others are nice. Raj is funny. Karen talks a lot, but she knows everything. I'm learning loads."

"What about the hours? You're up early, aren't you?"

"It's a six-o'clock start for breakfast prep."

"And the accommodation? Freddie said he'd sorted out a room for you."

"It's tiny. Literally just a bed and a wardrobe. But it's warm and it's mine." Kaylee paused. "It's better than I had this time last year."

"I'm glad you're settled. But if you need anything – better bedding, a lamp, whatever – just say, and I'll sort it."

"I'm fine, honestly. It's only for a short time, anyway."

"The offer still stands. I want you to be comfortable." Charlotte picked up her pen again. "Do any of the kitchen staff seem suspicious? Is anyone close to Brooke, for example?"

Kaylee thought for a moment. "Not really. Donna moans about him. Karen remembers the old society, but doesn't seem to know much about what's happening now. Raj just keeps his head down and gets on with his job."

"So, these sweet treats the kitchen has to provide for the chapel meetings… When are they held?"

"Wednesday evenings, usually. Sometimes on Saturdays. Donna said the next one's this Saturday."

Charlotte's eyes narrowed. "This Saturday? What time?"

"She starts prepping at six and delivers the food by seven. The meeting runs for a couple of hours, she thinks."

"That lines up with what we've seen – the login patterns from the music room."

Kaylee leaned forward. "Do you think that's where they're meeting, then?" she murmured. "The old music room?"

"I think so. I've planted bugs in there. If they do meet on Saturday, we'll hear everything."

"Bugs?" Kaylee grinned. "That's proper spy stuff."

"Something like that." Charlotte smiled, then her face grew serious again. "You're doing brilliantly, by the way. Thank you."

Kaylee shrugged. "Just returning the favour."

"It's more than that. You're good at this."

Kaylee felt a rush of pride. A year ago, she'd been convinced her life was over. Now she was helping solve a case, making a difference. It felt good. "I'll keep digging," she said.

"Just be careful. Whoever's behind this could be dangerous."

"I will." Kaylee stood up to leave, then paused. "Charlotte?"

"Yeah?"

"Thanks for everything. Not just this: the job and the room. I mean, last year. Getting me off the streets. I don't think I ever properly said thank you."

Charlotte's expression softened. "You don't need to thank me, Kaylee. You did the hard work; you got yourself sorted. I just helped."

"Still, I owe you."

"Kaylee, you don't owe me anything. But if you want to keep helping with cases like this, I won't say no."

Kaylee smiled. "Deal."

She left the staffroom and headed to her tiny room. She had a lot to think about. A secret society. A rogue teacher. Boys being hurt. She'd never thought twice about children in a private school before now, and she'd never imagined how utterly messed up the whole thing actually was.

Whatever was going on at St Athelstan's, Freddie had been right to hire them to investigate.

CHAPTER 23

Later that evening, Charlotte and Angus were in their flat. He was making tea in the tiny kitchen.

"I spoke to Kaylee," Charlotte said, as she lounged on the sofa. "She's heard about the secret society. The Apollonian Society."

Angus brought over two mugs and sat beside her. "What did she say?"

Charlotte relayed what Kaylee had told her: Karen's story about the society being shut down in the eighties, Brooke's chapel meetings, the food orders for senior boys.

"That could be the group we saw last night," Angus said. "In the music block."

"That's what I'm thinking. Secret meetings late at night, with limited membership. It certainly fits. Although, Brooke wasn't there..."

"Maybe they meet with and without him."

Charlotte considered this, then nodded. "Either way, the bugs I planted this morning should tell us. They're audio only, but that's all we need. They're transmitting to my laptop now. Next time they meet, we'll hear everything."

"When do you think that'll be?"

Charlotte pulled out her phone and checked her notes. "According to the login patterns, Admin_JEvans accesses the music block computer every Wednesday and Saturday night. So if the pattern holds, they'll be back tomorrow."

"Saturday night. What time?"

"Around eleven. It doesn't matter, anyway; it alerts me when it picks something up."

Angus took a sip of tea. "Well, at least we'll find out what they're really doing."

Charlotte nodded. "And if it's the society, we'll finally know what Brooke is up to."

There was a knock at the door. Angus answered it, and Freddie came in. He looked even more exhausted than usual, and dropped onto the sofa with a heavy sigh.

"Long day?" Angus asked, making a cup of tea and handing it to him.

"Long week. Long month." Freddie took the tea gratefully. "I only just got your message to meet. What did you want to talk about?"

Charlotte moved to the desk chair, turning it to face them. "Mr Brooke."

Freddie's expression didn't change, but he narrowed his eyes. "What about him?"

"We've heard he runs some kind of group," said Angus. "Dinner meetings. Chapel meetings. For select boys."

"Ah." Freddie took a sip of tea. "Yes. I know about those."

Angus leaned forward. "You do?"

"Of course. He requested permission when I first became headmaster. It's an enrichment programme for boys applying to Oxford and Cambridge."

Charlotte frowned. "Enrichment?"

"Academic support. Advice on applications, interview preparation, that sort of thing. Brooke went to Oxford himself: he read classics at Magdalen. He's well-connected, knows what the admissions tutors are looking for."

"And the special catering?" Charlotte asked.

Freddie nodded. "That's part of it. He wanted to make it feel special. Like a proper Oxford tutorial. Food, discussion, that sort of thing. Very traditional."

"Seems expensive," Angus said.

"Not really. Brooke funds most of it himself. Or rather, some of the alumni do. They're keen to see boys from St Athelstan's getting into Oxbridge." Freddie set his mug down. "Look, I know how it sounds. Secret meetings, select group of boys. But it's not sinister. It's just Mr Brooke trying to help."

"Why the secrecy?" Charlotte asked.

"It's not secret. Any boy can apply to join if they're serious about Oxbridge. But Mr Brooke only takes a handful each year, the ones he thinks have a genuine chance. He doesn't want to waste time on boys who aren't committed."

"And you trust him?" Angus asked.

Freddie looked at him for a long moment. "Mr Brooke has been a member of staff at this school for twenty years. He's one of our best teachers. Parents love him, boys respect him. Yes, I trust him."

"Even with everything that's been going on?" Charlotte pressed. "Teachers leaving, boys getting hurt, Oliver in hospital?"

Freddie rubbed his face. "I've considered it, of course I have. But there's no evidence linking Mr Brooke to any of that. And frankly, the Oxbridge programme is one of the few things going right at this school. Three of our boys secured places at Cambridge last year. That's a big deal."

Charlotte sat back. "So you don't think there's anything suspicious about these meetings?"

"I think..." Freddie paused, choosing his words carefully. "I think Mr Brooke is passionate about his subject and about getting boys into top universities. Is he a bit intense about it? Yes. Does he play favourites with the boys he thinks are

Oxbridge material? Probably. But that doesn't make him dangerous."

"What about the pressure on the boys?" Angus asked. "If they're not performing, if they don't get in?"

"True," Freddie admitted. "The Oxbridge application process is brutal. Lots of pressure. And yes, private-school students have a harder time now. There's a big push for state-school kids, widening participation, all that. So the bar's even higher for our boys. But if you're asking whether I think Brooke's programme is connected to Oliver's suicide attempt, I honestly don't think so. Oliver was in the group, yes. He was applying to read music at Oxford. But he dropped out of the programme about a month before the suicide attempt happened."

"He dropped out?" Charlotte asked.

"Yes. Brooke mentioned it to me. He said that Oliver had decided not to apply after all. Too much pressure, apparently. Brooke was disappointed, but understanding."

"Then a month later, Oliver tries to kill himself," Angus said quietly.

Freddie met his gaze. "I know how it looks, but correlation isn't causation. Oliver could have been struggling with all sorts of things. Depression, anxiety, family pressure ... we don't know. He's still not talking about it to anyone."

They sat in silence for a moment.

"Look," Freddie said, "I'm not dismissing your concerns. If you think there's something off about Mr Brooke or his programme, keep digging. But be careful. Mr Brooke is popular and well-respected. If you start making accusations without evidence, it could backfire badly."

"We're not making accusations," Charlotte said. "We're just observing."

"Good." Freddie stood up. "Keep observing. But also keep an open mind. Sometimes a cigar is just a cigar, you know?"

After Freddie had left, Charlotte turned to Angus. "He's not wrong. We don't have any hard evidence."

"But we have suspicious patterns," Angus said. "Oliver was in Brooke's group, left, then ended up in hospital. Davies was angry about not being picked. Harrison *was* picked, and looked scared when Oliver's name came up."

"And then there are the boys meeting secretly in the music block at night," Charlotte added. "Though we haven't told Freddie about that."

"There's no point until we know what they're doing."

Charlotte pulled up her laptop. "The bugs are active. If they meet tomorrow night, we'll hear everything."

"What about the encrypted files?"

"I'm still working on them. But I'm getting closer."

Angus stood up and stretched. "So we wait."

"We wait," Charlotte agreed. "But we keep watching Brooke. Freddie might trust him, but I don't."

"Neither do I." Angus walked to the window, looking out over the dark playing fields.

Charlotte closed her laptop. "Tomorrow night. We'll know more then."

"What if the boys in the music room are just studying? Just helping each other?"

"Then we'll cross them off the list and focus on Brooke. And Evans. And whoever's sending encrypted messages to Russia." Charlotte smiled grimly. "We've got plenty of other leads."

Angus turned from the window. "This school's a mess."

CHAPTER 24

Angus blew the whistle for the end of the warm-up drills. Year 11 again. Wednesday morning, overcast but dry. Good conditions for football.

"Right, lads, five-a-side. Same as last week. Split yourselves into teams."

The boys divided up quickly, grabbing bibs, setting up cones for goals. Angus watched them, noting who took charge, who hung back. Last week, Mark Harrison had stood out as vocal and confident. Today he stood to the side, hands in his pockets, staring at the ground.

"Harrison? You playing or what?"

Harrison looked up, startled. "Yeah. Sorry, sir." He jogged over to one of the teams, but his movements were sluggish.

Angus blew the whistle to start. The game began, fast and competitive. But within five minutes, it was clear something was wrong with Harrison.

He was slow. Reactive rather than proactive. The ball came to him and he hesitated, lost it to a defender. A simple pass went astray. He jogged when he should have sprinted.

One of his teammates shouted at him. "Come on, Harrison! Wake up!"

Harrison didn't respond. He kept moving mechanically, as if he was going through the motions.

Angus watched him carefully and came to a conclusion. This wasn't laziness. This was exhaustion.

After twenty minutes, Harrison stumbled, righted himself, then bent over with his hands on his knees, breathing hard.

Angus jogged over. "You all right?"

"Yeah, fine." But Harrison's face was pale and his hands trembled.

"When did you last eat?"

"Breakfast."

"Did you actually eat, or push food around your plate?"

Harrison didn't answer.

"Sit out for a bit," Angus said. "Get some water."

"I'm fine, sir."

"Sit it out. That's not a request."

Harrison straightened up. For a moment he looked as if he might argue, then nodded and walked over to the sidelines. He sat on the grass, pulled his knees up, and stared at nothing.

Angus let the game continue but kept an eye on Harrison. Should he send him to Matron? The boy didn't move. Didn't drink water. Just sat there, shoulders hunched.

When Angus blew the whistle for the end of the lesson, the other boys headed for the changing rooms, loud and cheerful. Harrison stayed where he was.

Angus walked over. "Harrison, I'd like a word."

The boy looked up, panic flashing across his face. "I didn't do anything wrong, sir."

"I know. I just want a word."

Harrison stood up slowly.

"You don't look well. Are you sleeping?"

"I'm fine."

"That's the second time you've said that, and I don't

believe you this time either." Angus folded his arms. "What's going on?"

Harrison's jaw tightened. "Nothing."

"You were one of the best players in this class last week. Today you could barely keep up. That's not nothing."

Harrison looked away. "I'm just tired."

"Why?"

"I don't know. I just am."

Angus studied the dark circles under his eyes. Then he noticed a tremor in his hands.

"Are you taking something?"

Harrison's head snapped up. "What?"

"You tell me. Study drugs? Caffeine pills? Something illegal?"

For a moment, Harrison looked terrified. Then he recovered and shook his head. "No, sir."

"Right." Angus didn't believe him, but pushing harder wouldn't help. "Look, if you need to talk to someone – Matron, the headmaster, me, anyone – you should. Whatever's going on, you don't have to deal with it alone."

Harrison's expression crumpled for just a second. Then he pulled it back together. "I'm fine, sir. Just need to sleep more. That's all."

"All right. But if this carries on, I'll have to speak to your housemaster."

Harrison loped off.

After the lesson, Angus did a routine check of the changing rooms. The usual debris remained: a wet towel on the floor, a forgotten water bottle.

He walked between the benches, checking for anything left behind. Phones, watches, that sort of thing. Boys were always forgetting things.

Then he saw something poking out from under a small plastic bottle, half-hidden under one of the benches. He pulled it out: a blister pack of tablets. He turned it over and read the writing on the metallic side: Modafinil 200mg.

It was nearly empty. Just three tablets were left.

He finished his check of the changing room, then locked up and headed to Matron's office. He found her eating a sandwich at her desk.

"Quick question," Angus said, closing the door behind him. "Study drugs. Is that a thing here?"

Mrs Hodge looked up, surprised. "Yeah. It's a bit of a problem, actually. Why?"

"I found some tablets in the changing room."

Matron sighed. "Modafinil? Ritalin?"

"Modafinil."

"Yeah, that's the one they all use. Keeps you awake, helps you focus. University students take it during exams. Some of the boys here have got hold of it."

"How?"

She shrugged. "The internet, probably. The headmaster's trying to crack down on it, but it's hard to police."

She took another bite of her sandwich. "None of the boys have been prescribed this. All prescriptions have to come through me, so I'd know if it was official."

"It was one of the year 11s. I suspect Harrison."

"Harrison? I wouldn't have thought he'd be using anything. Why do you think it's him?"

"He was overtired during football and had to sit out. I noticed his hands shaking afterwards."

"Next time, send him to me. I'll go and check on him now, though. Do you have the packet?"

Angus handed her the blister pack. "Thanks. I'll log it as an incident."

Angus left the office and headed back to the flat. Charlotte would want to know about this.

CHAPTER 25

On Saturday night Charlotte sat at the desk in the flat, laptop open and headphones on. Angus was beside her with his own set of earbuds. The audio software showed a flat green line, meaning silence in the music block.

It was ten forty-five. If the pattern held, the boys would arrive soon.

"You think they'll show?" Angus asked quietly.

"We'll know soon enough."

They waited. Charlotte refreshed the decryption software running in the background, still grinding away at the encrypted server.

At three minutes past eleven, the green line spiked. Charlotte's pulse quickened. "Movement."

She adjusted the audio levels. The sound of a door opening, then footsteps. Multiple people entering.

"Shut the door properly," a voice said. Teenage, authoritative. "Make sure it's locked."

There was a scuffling sound. More footsteps. Chairs scraping. Someone coughed.

"Where's Mitchell?" the same voice said.

"He couldn't get away. Someone's watching him."

Charlotte and Angus exchanged a glance.

"All right," the first voice said. "Let's start. We don't have long."

A pause, then, "What's new with Oliver?"

Silence. Then a quieter voice, "My mum spoke to his mum. He's talking now. Not much, but he's talking."

"What's he saying?"

"Nothing about what happened. Just normal stuff. The doctors, the food, that sort of thing."

"He's too scared," another boy said. "Even after everything, he's still too scared to say anything."

"Can you blame him?" The authoritative voice again. "Look what happened to him. He tried to tell someone, and they destroyed him. If Oliver talks now, they'll make sure everyone knows what he did. His parents, the university, everyone. Oliver's life is over, either way."

They. Not a specific name.

"We need to be smarter than Oliver," the authoritative boy continued. "We can't just go to someone and hope for the best. We need evidence, real evidence. Something they can't talk their way out of."

"Like what?" someone asked.

"I don't know. Records, maybe. Emails. Something that proves what's been going on."

"Good luck with that," another boy said. "They're not stupid. They don't write things down."

"Then we record them. Get them on tape saying something incriminating."

"How? They're not going to confess to us."

"Is Harrison still in?" someone asked quietly.

"Yeah. They have too much on him. He can't get out."

"None of us can get out," a bitter voice said. "That's the whole point. Once you're in, you're stuck. They make sure of it."

"So what do we do?" a younger voice asked.

"We gather information. Quietly, carefully. We watch who's being targeted, who's meeting with them. We write it all down. Dates, times, who was there. And when we have enough, we take it to someone who can actually do something about it."

"Like who? The headmaster? I bet he's in on it too. We can't trust anyone."

"Nah, he's clueless. I don't think he's in on it, but we can't trust him. Not yet."

"What about the police? Someone will listen if we have enough evidence."

"And what do we do in the meantime?"

"We look out for each other. If they approach any of us, we tell the group. If someone's struggling, we help them. We stick together. That's the only way we'll survive this."

There was a murmur of agreement.

"What about the new teachers, Mr and Mrs Harper?" the younger boy asked again. "Could we talk to them?"

The leader hesitated. "Mrs Hacker and Mr Whistler? We don't know if we can trust them."

"They could be part of it," the bitter voice countered. "Maybe they're here because someone asked for them."

Another pause.

"All right," the leader said. "Keep an eye on them. See if they ask any more questions."

"Agreed."

"Anything else?" the leader asked.

"Yeah," someone said. "Davies is still angry about not getting picked for Brooke's group. He's been making noise, saying it's not fair."

"Let him. At least he's safe. Better to be angry about not being picked than stuck like Harrison."

"True."

More murmurs of agreement.

"Right," the leader said. "Time to go. One at a time, five minutes apart, same as always. And remember – no phones, no emails, nothing. They could be monitoring anything."

"Understood."

Charlotte pulled off her headphones. Angus did the same.

They stared at each other until Angus spoke. "Mrs Hacker and Mr Whistler?"

"What?"

"That's what the boys call us. Mrs Hacker and Mr Whistler. You heard them."

Charlotte smiled despite the gravity of what they'd just listened to. "Mrs Hacker. I like it."

"You would."

"Mr Whistler's not bad either. Very distinguished. Like the painter."

"It's because I blow a whistle, Charlotte. Not because I paint." He shook his head. "Anyway, that's not the point. One of those boys thinks we're trustworthy. That could be useful."

"Or dangerous. If the wrong person finds out the boys are thinking about talking to us, it could put them at risk."

"Agreed. We let them come to us. No pushing. They never said who 'they' are," Angus said.

"No. Just 'they.' Not Brooke, specifically."

"But Mark Harrison's involved. Oliver was. And whoever's behind it has something on the boys. Blackmail material?"

Charlotte replayed parts of the recording in her head. "They said 'they destroyed him.' Not 'Brooke destroyed him.' Just 'they.'"

"It could be multiple people," Angus said. "Or they're being careful not to say names in case someone's listening."

"Smart, if that's the case."

Angus stood up and stretched. "The music-block boys aren't the problem. They're the victims."

"Whatever this operation is, escaping it costs something."

Charlotte saved the audio recording and backed it up to three different locations. "This is evidence. The boys talked about being blackmailed, about Oliver being destroyed. If we can combine this with whatever's in the encrypted server..."

"We can stop whoever's behind it."

Charlotte looked at Angus. "They're just kids. Teenagers trying to protect each other because the adults won't. It's awful."

"Freddie doesn't know how bad it is. And the other teachers either haven't noticed or don't want to get involved."

Charlotte thought for a moment. "We need to be careful. If we approach them directly, they might panic. And if whoever's behind this finds out we're talking to them..."

"The leader," Angus said. "Did you recognise the voice?"

Charlotte shook her head. "He sounded older. Sixth form, probably. What now?"

"I need you to bug the chapel and the room where Brooke has his meetings. We need to find out what's going on in those."

Charlotte smiled. "Consider it done."

CHAPTER 26

That night, Charlotte went through the school's room-booking system. She pulled up the chapel booking schedule. There it was: *Brooke - Oxbridge Study Group - Sunday 7-9pm - Chapel Side Room.*

There would be another meeting the next day.

She checked her bag: there were two audio bugs left from the set Grigore had given her. She'd used two in the music block. These two would have to do for now, but she could get more soon.

She glanced at her watch: eleven thirty. The chapel would be quiet now, and the whole school should be in bed. She could wait until tomorrow morning or afternoon, but there was more chance of being discovered. The chapel would be in frequent use, tomorrow being Sunday. Angus was already asleep. She could leave, get the job done quickly and head back.

She grabbed her bag and a torch and slipped out of the flat.

The school was eerily silent. Charlotte hurried along until the chapel loomed ahead of her. She went through the main door and slipped in, closing the door quietly behind her.

The chapel was beautiful even in darkness. Old stone, stained-glass windows barely visible even with moonlight filtering through them. Carved wooden pews either side of the centre. It smelled of candles, old hymn books, and dust.

Charlotte had only been inside once, during Freddie's tour. Now, in the darkness, it felt different. Larger, more imposing.

She pulled out her torch, keeping the beam low. Her footsteps echoed as she walked down the centre aisle. At the front, to the left of the altar, was a small door. She tried the handle.

It was unlocked.

The side room was smaller than she'd expected. A round table sat in the middle with eight chairs around it. Bookshelves lined one wall: theology texts, philosophy, classical literature. This had to be where Brooke held his meetings.

Charlotte pulled out the first bug and looked around. It needed to be close to the table, but hidden.

She crouched down and stuck the bug under the table, near the centre. There should be good audio pickup from there.

She heard a sound and froze.

Footsteps, coming closer.

She switched off her torch, plunging the room into darkness.

The footsteps continued.

She crept to the door and peered through the crack. A figure was backlit by moonlight from the windows. Tall, male, moving towards the altar.

The figure stopped at the front pew and stood there for a moment, completely still. Then he knelt.

Charlotte exhaled slowly. Just someone praying.

She stayed frozen, waiting.

The figure remained kneeling, head bowed. One minute. Two.

She shifted slightly, trying to stay silent.

The figure stood up and turned.

For a moment, they seemed to look straight at the side room door. Charlotte's heart banged in her chest.

But then the figure walked back down the aisle, footsteps echoing. The main chapel door opened, then closed.

Silence.

Charlotte waited a full minute, listening. Nothing. Whoever it was had gone.

She switched her torch back on, hands shaking slightly. She needed to finish and get out.

She placed the second bug behind one of the bookshelves, tucked between two large volumes of Plato. Then she checked her phone. Both bugs were active, transmitting clearly.

Now, all she wanted was to be back in bed with Angus, safe and secure.

She moved to the side-room door and listened. Nothing. The chapel was silent again.

She slipped out, closed the door quietly, and hurried down the aisle.

At the main door, she paused. Had it been locked from the outside?

She tried the handle. It turned.

Back through the corridors, past the silent classrooms, up the stairs to their flat.

Only when she was inside, with the door locked and bolted behind her, did she allow herself to relax. The school was eerie, and, she could admit it to herself, scary at night.

Angus was asleep, his breathing steady and regular. Charlotte sat on the edge of the bed, her heart still racing.

That had been far too close for comfort. If whoever it was had come into the side room, had seen her there…

But they hadn't. The bugs were in place. Tomorrow night, they'd hear everything Brooke said to his students. Then they'd know for certain whether he was innocent or involved.

Charlotte got changed quietly and slid into bed beside Angus. She lay in the darkness, replaying the episode in her head. The figure kneeling, the silence, the footsteps.

Who could it have been? A teacher? A student? Someone who couldn't sleep?

She pushed the thought away. Paranoia wouldn't help. The bugs were in place. Tomorrow, they'd have answers.

She closed her eyes and tried to sleep.

CHAPTER 27

On Sunday evening, Charlotte and Angus sat at the desk again, headphones on, laptop open. The audio feed from the chapel was live.

At just after seven o'clock, the first sounds came through. A door opening. Footsteps.

"Good evening, everyone." An adult voice, cultured, warm. Mr Brooke.

"Evening, sir." Multiple boys' voices.

"Right, let's get started. Help yourselves to a drink and a cake first. We've got a lot to cover tonight."

There were sounds of chairs scraping, mugs clinking, the rustle of papers.

After a few minutes, Brooke spoke again: "Where did we leave off last week? Ah, yes, Michaelmas term applications. Who has already submitted their UCAS form?"

"I have, sir." A boy's voice, confident.

"Excellent, Thomas. Anyone else?"

"Mine's nearly done, sir," said another boy. "Just tweaking the conclusion."

"Good. Remember, your personal statement needs to show

passion for the subject, not just academic achievement. They want to see why you're excited about law, or classics, or whatever you're applying for."

"Yes, sir."

Brooke continued. "Now, interview preparation. Cambridge interviews are notoriously tough. They're not testing what you know; they're testing how you think. Christopher, let's start with you. You're applying for natural sciences. I'll ask you a question, and I want you to talk me through your reasoning. Don't worry about getting the right answer; just show me your thought process."

"Okay, sir."

"Right. Here's the question: Why is the sky blue?"

A pause. Then Christopher's voice: "Er, because of the way sunlight scatters in the atmosphere?"

"Good start. But why does it scatter? And why blue, specifically?"

Christopher thought aloud, working through the physics. Brooke listened, occasionally asking follow-up questions, guiding him towards the answer.

Charlotte glanced at Angus. He was listening intently.

This was just teaching.

Brooke moved on to the next boy. "Harrison, you're applying for engineering. Here's your question: How would you design a bridge to cross a valley?"

Harrison's voice was quieter, hesitant. "Um … I'd need to know how wide the valley is."

"Good. What else?"

"The depth. What materials I have available."

"Excellent. Keep going."

Harrison talked through the problem, his voice gaining confidence as he worked. Brooke encouraged him, asked clarifying questions, pushed him to think deeper.

For the next hour, Charlotte and Angus listened as Brooke

worked through interview questions with each boy. He was patient, encouraging, insightful. He corrected them when they went off-track, praised them when they made good points.

At eight fifteen, Brooke called a break. "Right, ten minutes. Stretch your legs, more drinks if you want them."

The sound of chairs scraping, boys talking quietly among themselves.

Then Brooke's voice again, closer to the table. "Harrison, can I have a quick word?"

"Yes, sir."

A pause. Then Brooke spoke quietly: "Are you all right? You seem distracted tonight."

"I'm fine, sir."

"You don't look fine. You look exhausted. Are you sleeping?"

"Not much, sir. Just stressed about applications and exams."

"I understand that, but you need to look after yourself. No university is worth making yourself ill over. If you need to talk to someone – Matron, the headmaster, or me – then you should."

"I'm okay, sir. Really."

"All right. But I'm keeping an eye on you. You're one of my best students, Harrison. I don't want to see you burn out."

"Thank you, sir."

Charlotte and Angus looked at each other. Brooke sounded genuinely concerned.

The meeting resumed. More interview prep, more discussion of personal statements.

At nine o'clock, Brooke wrapped up. "That's enough for tonight. Keep working on your statements. I want drafts from all of you by Friday. And Harrison, get some sleep."

"Yes, sir."

The boys filed out. The door closed. Silence.

Charlotte pulled off her headphones. Angus did the same. "That was completely innocent," Angus said.

"Completely. He's just teaching them. Preparing them for interviews."

"And he's worried about Harrison. Asked if he was okay."

Charlotte leaned back in her chair. "Brooke doesn't know. He has no idea what's happening to his students. He isn't the one doing it."

"No. He's just running a legitimate Oxbridge programme."

They sat in silence for a moment.

"So who is?" Angus asked. "The music-block boys kept saying 'they' destroyed Oliver. If it's not Brooke, who is it?"

Charlotte thought for a moment. "Could be another teacher. Someone using Brooke's programme as cover."

"Like who?"

"I don't know. We should even consider Matron."

"But why would they target Brooke's students?"

Charlotte frowned. "Access? Trust? The boys are already meeting late, already on computers; plus, if they're applying to Oxbridge, they'll be the top students."

"That doesn't narrow it down much. Half the staff could have access to those boys."

"We need to watch the other staff and the older boys in year 13: they could be preying on the younger ones. But I want to look into Jeremy Evans too. I don't know why, but Evans just doesn't feel right."

"Gut feeling?" Angus smiled. "Spoken like a true detective. But we checked him out. Grigore went to his office. It looked completely legitimate."

"Maybe that's the point. The perfect cover: a respectable businessman who employs disabled people and has an OBE. No one would suspect him."

Angus pondered. "He has access to the entire school

network. He could monitor everything: emails, files, which students are doing well academically. He'd know exactly which boys to target. But it's just a hypothesis. All the other staff do too."

Charlotte thought for a moment. "We can dig a bit deeper and find out once and for all. The encrypted files will help. But we need something more concrete. Something that directly links Evans to what's happening. Or not."

"Like what?"

"I could create a virus that crashes part of the school network. Something urgent enough that Evans has to come in person to fix it. Then I talk to him, see how he reacts. And..." Charlotte paused, thinking. "And I plant a bug on him."

Angus shook his head. "I'm not sure. You know how I feel about things like this. It's one thing to place bugs here in the school, where we've been asked to investigate, but it's another to plant them on someone."

Charlotte opened a drawer in the desk and pulled out a device no bigger than a button. "New supplies! An audio bug. Same type I used in the music block. I could attach it to his laptop bag, his coat, his car. Anywhere he won't notice."

"When would you have the chance?"

"When he's fixing the network. I could say I need to show him something and get him to come to our flat or the computer suite. While he's distracted, I'll plant it."

Angus considered this. "It's risky. If he realises what you're doing..."

"He won't. I'll be careful." Charlotte checked the time. Nine thirty. "I'll deploy the virus tomorrow morning. Something that looks like a legitimate network failure, but requires urgent attention. Evans will have to come in."

"And if he doesn't come? If he tries to fix it remotely?"

"I'll make sure he can't. The virus will be designed to require physical access to the server."

Angus nodded. "All right. But if this goes wrong—"

"It won't go wrong."

"Charlotte…"

She looked at him. "I'll be careful, I promise. I think we should speak to Kaylee so that she knows what we've found."

"All right. Text her to come to the flat. Then we can talk without worrying about being overheard."

CHAPTER 28

Kaylee sat on the sofa, clutching a mug of tea. Angus sat beside her, Charlotte at the desk. The door was locked, curtains drawn.

"Right," Angus said. "Let's go through everything we know."

He pulled out his phone and opened his notes. "Harrison. Year 11, one of Brooke's Oxbridge students. Exhausted, can't concentrate, hands shaking. I found Modafinil in the changing room: a study drug. Matron confirmed it's common with the Oxbridge boys. I've no proof that Harrison's using it, but my instinct says it's him. There could be others."

"How bad did he look?" Kaylee asked.

"Bad. Like he hadn't slept properly in days."

Charlotte nodded. "On Saturday night we listened to the audio from the music block. Six or seven boys are meeting in secret. They're not the problem. They're trying to protect each other."

Kaylee's eyes widened. "Protect each other from what?"

"That's what we don't know," Angus said. "They talked about Oliver. The boys said he tried to get out of something and 'they' destroyed him. But they never said who 'they' were."

"And they said Harrison's still trapped," Charlotte added. "That someone has something on him, so he can't leave."

Kaylee set her mug down. "So someone's blackmailing students?"

"Yes, but we can't figure out who." Charlotte pulled up her laptop. "Last night, I bugged Brooke's official Oxbridge meeting in the chapel. We listened to the whole thing."

Kaylee leaned forward. "And?"

"It was completely innocent," Angus said. "Brooke was just teaching them. Interview preparation, personal statements. He even noticed that Harrison looked exhausted and told him to get some sleep."

"So Brooke isn't behind it?" Kaylee said.

"No. He's just running a legitimate programme." Charlotte opened a file on her laptop. "Which means we have to figure out who else it could be. Our next focus of attention is Jeremy Evans."

"Who's that?" Kaylee asked.

"The IT contractor. He has access to the entire school network. He can monitor everything, see which students are doing well academically, which ones are in Brooke's programme. He has the perfect way to identify targets. I'm going to deploy a virus onto the network which means that he'll have to come in to fix it."

"Have you got anything?" Angus asked Kaylee.

Kaylee nodded. "Yesterday, I was cleaning tables in the refectory after lunch. Most people had left, but there were two year 12 boys at a table in the corner. They didn't see me: I was behind one of those big serving trolleys."

"What were they saying?" Charlotte asked.

"They were arguing. One of them – tall, dark hair, prefect badge – he was saying something like, 'You need to keep going, we're almost done.' The other one, shorter, looked really stressed. He said, 'I can't do this any more. If anyone finds out…'"

"Did you recognise either of the boys?" Charlotte asked.

Kaylee shook her head. "I don't know names yet. The tall one was a prefect: he had the badge. Dark hair, looked like a rugby player. The shorter one was blond, thin, looked like he hadn't slept in days." She paused. "What can I do?" she said. "I want to help."

"You've already helped," said Charlotte.

"But I want to do more," Kaylee insisted. "These boys aren't much younger than me. Someone needs to stop whoever's behind this."

Charlotte glanced at Angus, then back at Kaylee. "How comfortable would you be with planting a bug?"

"A listening device?"

"Yes. Small, magnetic. You just put it somewhere Evans won't notice. In his laptop bag, on his coat."

Kaylee nodded. "I can do that."

"It might be risky," Angus warned. "If he catches you—"

"He won't," Kaylee said. "I'm invisible in this place. No one pays attention to the kitchen staff. I can bring him tea, ask if he needs anything, get close without him suspecting."

Charlotte pulled a magnetic audio bug from her desk drawer. "This is what you'd be planting."

Kaylee took the bug and turned it over in her hand. "How does it work?"

"It transmits audio to my laptop."

"And if he finds it?"

"It's small enough that he probably won't. Even if he does, there's no way to trace it back to us."

Kaylee looked at Charlotte, then Angus. "All right. I'll do it."

"You're sure?" Angus asked.

"I'm sure. You helped me when I had nothing. This is how I pay you back."

Charlotte smiled. "Thank you, Kaylee."

"So what's the plan?" Kaylee asked.

"Tomorrow morning, I deploy the virus," Charlotte said. "The network crashes, Evans gets called in. While he's fixing the server I'll try to get him talking, see if I can get anything incriminating. You'll be nearby, maybe bringing refreshments to the IT room. When you get the chance, plant the bug. His coat, his bag, wherever works."

"And then?" Kaylee asked.

"Then we listen. See who he talks to. If he contacts the boys or makes any calls, we'll hear."

Kaylee pocketed the bug. "What time will things start tomorrow?"

"Early, around seven thirty. The virus will trigger during the morning login rush. Maximum chaos, maximum urgency."

Kaylee smiled. "I'll be ready."

CHAPTER 29

Monday morning, five forty. Charlotte slipped out of the flat, leaving Angus asleep. She'd set her alarm for five thirty, silenced it before it could wake him. He'd stirred briefly as she'd got out of bed but hadn't woken. He always slept so soundly. She envied his ability to fall asleep quickly and stay asleep all night.

She'd packed a small bag with her set of lockpicks, a tiny camera, and her phone. The camera was barely larger than a coin, wireless, high-definition. It would transmit directly to her laptop.

The science corridor felt darker than the rest of the school. There were no windows, just stone walls and locked classroom doors. At the far end, the server-room door looked exactly as it had after her first visit.

Charlotte pulled out her lockpicks and worked the lock easily, then pushed the door open and slipped inside.

The single bare bulb cast harsh shadows across the cluttered room. Boxes of old paperwork, broken equipment, dusty shelves. And at the back, hidden behind the mess, the server rack with its expensive hardware.

Charlotte navigated the clutter and crouched in front of

the rack. The main server hummed quietly, status lights blinking. Below it was the mysterious second server, the one with no branding and a plain black case.

Charlotte pulled out the video camera and examined the rack, looking for the best position.

She needed a view of anyone who came into the room. Ideally, she wanted to see their face and see what they did with the servers. But the camera had to be hidden well enough that no one would spot it.

She looked up. Above the rack was a gap between the top of the equipment and the ceiling. Perfect.

She stood on an old office chair she'd dragged over and put the camera in the gap. The magnetic base held it in place. She angled it downwards, checking the view on her phone.

The camera covered the entire server rack and most of the floor space in front of it. Anyone working on the servers would be clearly visible.

She activated the camera. A green light blinked once, then went dark. It was live.

Charlotte climbed down from the chair and put it back where she'd found it. Then she took one last look at the camera. Invisible, unless you knew exactly where to look.

She checked her phone again. The video feed was coming through clearly.

She opened the door a crack and listened. Silence. The corridor was still empty.

She slipped out and headed to her flat. By the time she reached it, it was five fifty-five.

She sat down at the desk and opened her laptop. The video feed from the server room loaded immediately. Clear, high-definition, comprehensive. She wondered why she hadn't thought about putting a camera in there before.

When Evans came to fix the virus attack, they'd have him on camera. Every movement, every action, everything he did with those servers. Combined with the audio bug Kaylee would plant, they'd have complete surveillance. Video and audio.

Charlotte saved the feed settings and closed the laptop. She heard Angus stirring in the bed behind her.

"Morning," he mumbled, his voice thick with sleep. "What time is it?"

"About six. I woke early, couldn't get back to sleep."

Angus sat up, rubbing his eyes. "Nervous?"

"A bit."

"Camera in place?"

"Yes. Video feed's working perfectly."

Angus got out of bed and came over. Charlotte reopened the laptop and pulled up the feed. The server room appeared, slightly grainy but in clear detail.

"Good position," Angus said. "He won't see it?"

"Not unless he's looking for a camera. And why would he? He thinks the room's secure."

"Right." Angus glanced at the clock. "When are you uploading the virus?"

"I'm about to do it now." Charlotte turned to look at him. "Do you think we should tell Freddie?"

"Not for now. The fewer people who know, the better. Besides, although we're being employed here to find out what's going on, attacking a computer system with a virus is still illegal."

"He'll guess it's me, though, when he finds out."

"If he asks directly, tell him. Otherwise, we'll just let things take their natural course."

"Right." She tapped at the keyboard. "I've done it. It's a ransomware simulator. It'll look as if the main file server has been infected. Staff files, student records, everything will appear encrypted. But it isn't real. I can reverse it in seconds."

"And Evans will think it's a genuine attack?"

"Yes. It'll trigger every security alert he has. Server down, files encrypted, urgent response required. He'll have to come in to assess the damage and fix it."

Angus was quiet for a moment. "What if he can tell it's fake?"

"He won't. I've made it look like a standard ransomware strain. A WannaCry variant. Same behaviour, same encryption patterns. There's an easy way to fix it, but he'll have to come in."

"And Kaylee's ready?"

"Yep. She'll be in the kitchen, waiting. As soon as Evans arrives, she'll bring him tea or coffee and get close enough to plant the bug."

CHAPTER 30

Charlotte and Angus arrived at the refectory, and the room was already filling with boys, the noise level rising as more students filtered in.

Charlotte and Angus headed to the counter for breakfast. Kaylee was serving, her face neutral as she spooned scrambled eggs onto plates.

"Morning," Charlotte said, as she reached the front.

"Morning, Mrs Harper." Kaylee's voice was perfectly professional.

Charlotte took her plate and sat at the staff table. Angus joined her a moment later. They ate in relative silence, surrounded by the chaos of two hundred boys having breakfast.

Around her, teachers were pulling out their phones, checking emails, preparing for the day. No one had noticed yet.

A few minutes later, Miss Hartley frowned at her phone. "That's odd. My lesson plans aren't loading."

Mr Sandbrook, the nervous head of geography, tried his tablet. "Mine aren't either. Is the network down?"

More teachers pulled out their devices. Murmurs of confusion spread along the table. Charlotte kept her expression neutral and took another bite of toast.

Mrs Hodge, the matron, appeared in the refectory doorway, looking flustered. She scanned the room, spotted Charlotte, and walked quickly over. "Mrs Harper. Sorry to interrupt your breakfast, but—"

Charlotte looked up. "Morning, Mrs Hodge. Is everything all right?"

"Not really, no. Something's wrong with the computers. All the staff files are showing up as encrypted, the secretary can't access anything, and there's a message on every computer screen saying something about a virus." She shook her head. "You're the computing teacher, can you help?"

Charlotte tried her best to look concerned. "I could have a look, but I'm afraid I won't be much help. I just teach the basics. Viruses, network security … that's not really my area. I wouldn't want to make things worse."

Mrs Hodge's face fell. "Oh. I thought that as you work with computers…"

"I can teach kids how to make spreadsheets, yes. But fixing a virus? That's way above my knowledge level." Charlotte gestured helplessly. "Have you contacted the IT contractor? The one who manages the school network? J. Evans, isn't it? He's the person who does all the technical stuff. You should tell the headmaster to call him. Urgently."

"Right. Yes. I'll go and find him now." Mrs Hodge hurried off.

Angus gave Charlotte the briefest of looks. Evans would be summoned.

Around the table, teachers were starting to panic. "I've got year 11 coursework to mark and it's all on the server."

"I can't see my lesson plans for the week; what am I supposed to do?"

"Is this one of those ransomware attacks? Like in the news?"

Freddie appeared in the doorway, Mrs Hodge hovering behind him. Both looked worried. Freddie pulled out his phone, tapped at it and walked quickly out of the refectory with it held to his ear.

Charlotte finished her breakfast, outwardly calm.

At nine o'clock, Charlotte stood in front of her year 9 computing class. Eighteen boys stared at blank computer screens.

"Good morning, everyone," Charlotte said. "As you've probably noticed, the computers aren't working this morning. There's a technical problem with the network. So we're going to do some theory instead."

There were groans from around the room.

"I know, I know, but this is important stuff. We're going to learn about binary."

More groans.

Charlotte went to the whiteboard and wrote: *BINARY TO DENARY CONVERSIONS*

"Binary is how computers store all information. Every number, every letter, every image is all just ones and zeros. Inside every computer are millions and sometimes billions of tiny on-off switches which can process those digits. Today, you'll learn how to convert binary numbers into normal denary, decimal, numbers."

She wrote on the board:

128 64 32 16 8 4 2 1

"These are place values in binary. Each position represents a power of two. So if I give you a binary number, such as 10110101, you can work out what it means in decimal."

One of the boys put his hand up. "Miss, why do we need to know this if the computers do it for us?"

"Because understanding how computers think makes you better at using them." She smiled. "And it's in the exam."

That got their attention.

She worked through several examples on the board,

the boys copying them into their exercise books. Some got the hang of it quickly. Others struggled but kept trying.

It was almost meditative, teaching without computers. Just whiteboard and pen, and students actually thinking rather than clicking.

Twenty minutes into the lesson, there was a knock on the door. Freddie entered, followed by a man Charlotte had never seen in person.

He was in his late thirties, lean, dressed in dark jeans and a casual blazer. Brown hair, clean-shaven, wire-rimmed glasses. He carried a laptop bag slung over one shoulder and had an air of calm competence about him.

"Sorry to interrupt, Mrs Harper," Freddie said. "This is Jeremy Evans, our IT contractor. He's going to try and fix the network. I thought he could work in here while you continue your lesson?"

"Of course," Charlotte said, keeping her voice neutral. So this was Evans. Finally. She assessed him. She'd seen his photo, of course; he'd been in all the papers when he'd received his OBE from the king a couple of years ago. He didn't look much older. "We're just doing some binary conversions," she said. "We won't be too noisy."

"Thanks." Freddie turned to Evans. "I'll leave you to it. Let me know when you've worked out what's happened."

Freddie left. Evans set his laptop bag on Charlotte's desk and pulled out a sleek MacBook Pro.

Charlotte looked at the boys, who had all turned to watch. "Right, back to work," she said firmly. "Question three is on the board. Convert 11010011 into decimal, showing your workings."

The boys turned back to their exercise books, though a few kept glancing at Evans.

Evans booted up his laptop and pulled out a network cable, connecting it to the wall socket. His fingers moved quickly over the keyboard, pulling up command prompts and network diagnostics.

Charlotte continued teaching, writing more binary numbers on the board, helping students who were stuck. But she was acutely aware of Evans working just a few metres away.

At ten, the bell rang and Charlotte ended the lesson. The boys closed their exercise books and filed out.

Charlotte walked over to her desk. Evans was still focused on his screen, frowning. "Any luck?" she asked.

Evans looked up. "Not yet. This is nasty. Looks like a WannaCry variant. Ransomware. It's encrypted all the files on the main server, and it's trying to spread to other machines."

"Is it serious?"

"Very. If I can't contain it, the whole network could be compromised. Student records, financial data, everything." He ran a hand through his hair. "I need to isolate the affected server and see if I can decrypt the files before they're lost permanently."

Charlotte leaned against the desk, keeping her expression concerned but not overly interested. "How do these things even happen? I thought schools had antivirus software."

"They do, but these attacks are sophisticated. Someone clicks on a dodgy email attachment, and boom, the whole network's infected." Evans turned back to his screen. "I'm running a trace now to see where it entered the system."

"Do you think you can fix it?"

"I hope so. If not, we might have to restore from backups. But that means losing the last few days of data. Staff won't be happy."

Charlotte nodded sympathetically. "Well, I'll leave you to it. I've got another class coming in ten minutes."

"Actually..." Evans said, still looking at his screen, "you're the computing teacher, right?"

"I am, yes."

"Do you know much about network security? Firewalls, that sort of thing?"

"Not really. I'm on the teaching side: a bit of basic programming and spreadsheets. I was an ICT teacher before the government changed the curriculum. I had to learn how to program one summer or get pushed out. The technical back-end stuff is beyond me. That's why we need someone like you."

Evans nodded. "Fair enough. I just thought I'd ask."

"Sorry I can't help."

"No worries." Evans unplugged his laptop and started packing it away. "I'd better get to the server room. I'll need physical access to isolate this properly."

"The server room's at the end of the science corridor, isn't it?"

"Yeah. It's a horrible little room full of junk, but that's where the school keeps the hardware." He slung his laptop bag over his shoulder. "Hopefully I can sort this out before lunchtime. Otherwise, it's going to be a long day."

"Good luck."

"Thanks." Evans gave her a brief smile and left.

Charlotte waited until his footsteps had faded down the corridor, then pulled out her phone.

The video feed from the server room was active. She checked the time. Evans would be there in less than two minutes.

She sent a text to Kaylee: *Evans heading to server room now. Camera ready.*

The reply came immediately: *Good. On my way.*

Charlotte sat down at her desk and opened her laptop, pulling up the video feed. The server room appeared on screen – empty, quiet, servers humming in the background.

CHAPTER 31

Kaylee stood in the small kitchen prep area just off the main refectory, arranging items on a tray. She'd volunteered to take refreshments to the server room, and no one had blinked an eye at the idea. "Shall I take the IT man some tea? They usually want tea, don't they, when they're working."

Donna had barely looked up. "Good thinking. Take some biscuits too. Digestives, custard creams, or a mix. We'd better keep him happy."

Now Kaylee had the tray ready: a mug of tea, a small jug of milk, a sugar bowl, and a plate of biscuits. Professional, helpful. Completely normal.

The audio bug was in her apron pocket. She'd checked it three times already. It was tiny and magnetic, ready to attach to anything made of metal.

Her hands were steady as she lifted the tray. She'd been more nervous a year ago, when she was homeless and desperate. This was different. She was doing this for something that mattered.

She left the kitchen and walked down the main corridor towards the science wing. A few students passed, barely glancing at the kitchen staff member carrying a tray. Invisible, just like she had told Charlotte.

The science corridor was quieter. Most classes were in session. Kaylee could hear a teacher's voice in one of the labs, saying something about chemical reactions.

At the end of the corridor, the server-room door stood slightly ajar. As she got closer, Kaylee heard equipment being moved and someone muttering under their breath.

She stopped just outside. "Mr Evans? I've brought you some tea."

The movement inside stopped, then, "Oh, thanks. Come in."

Kaylee opened the door with her foot and stepped inside.

The room was exactly as Charlotte had described: cluttered with old equipment and boxes of paperwork. At the back was Jeremy Evans, crouching in front of the server rack with his laptop open beside him.

He looked up as she entered. "Thanks for bringing me a drink. You didn't have to do that."

"We thought you might need it. Looks like you'll be here a while." Kaylee set down the tray on top of a filing cabinet, the only clear surface she could find.

"You're not wrong." Evans stood up, stretching his back. "This virus is a nightmare. Whoever designed it knew what they were doing."

Kaylee indicated the mug. "Milk? Sugar?"

"Just milk, thanks. Not too much."

She added a splash of milk, then walked over and handed him the mug. As he took it, she glanced at his laptop bag, sitting on the floor beside the server rack. It was made of black leather, expensive-looking. The front pocket was half unzipped.

"How long do you think it'll take?" she asked, keeping her voice conversational. "To fix it, I mean."

Evans took a sip of tea. "Hard to say. Could be an hour,

could be all day. Depends on how deep it goes." He put the mug down on a stack of boxes. "So, you work in the kitchen? I don't think I've seen you before."

"Yeah, I started last week."

"How are you finding it?"

"It's all right. The staff are nice. The boys are... Well, they're teenage boys." She smiled a little.

Evans chuckled. "Yeah, I bet. I did some work at another boarding school last year. The noise at mealtimes is unbelievable."

He turned back to his laptop and typed something, watching the screen.

Kaylee glanced at the laptop bag again. The front pocket was almost within reach. She just needed a reason to get closer. She could do this. She knew she could. Failure was not going to happen.

She took a small step forward, pretending to look at the server rack. "Is that what's infected? That big computer thing?"

"Yeah. This is the main file server. All the school's data runs through it." Evans gestured at the screen. "I'm trying to isolate the encrypted files and see if I can restore them from the backup."

Kaylee moved closer, as if trying to see the screen better. She was now standing right next to the laptop bag.

"It's all a bit complicated for me," she said, with a self-deprecating laugh. "I can use my phone and that's it. I've never really used a computer much."

Evans smiled, still looking at the screen of his laptop. "You're not alone. Most people don't understand how any of this works. They just know when it stops working."

"Oops, shoelace," Kaylee murmured, and crouched down next to the bag. As she retied her lace, she glanced up at Evans. He was completely absorbed in his screen. Her hand moved to her apron pocket, fingers closing around the audio bug.

In one smooth movement, Kaylee's hand moved to the laptop bag. The front pocket was open just enough and she slipped the bug inside, feeling it attach itself to the bag's metal frame.

She stood up quickly, brushing off her apron. "Well, I'll let you get on. Give me a shout if you need anything else. I'll leave the plate of biscuits."

"Thanks." Evans didn't look up.

Kaylee walked back to the filing cabinet, picked up the tray and headed for the door.

"Just a minute," Evans said.

Kaylee's heart missed a beat. She turned slowly. "Yes?"

Evans picked up the mug of tea and smiled. "Thanks for this. I really needed it."

"No problem."

She left the room, closing the door behind her. Only then did she allow herself to breathe out. As she walked back down the science corridor, her hands started to tremble a little.

She'd done it. The bug was in place. She couldn't help smiling.

By the time she reached the main corridor, her hands had steadied. She walked past a group of year 7 boys, heading to their next lesson. Her back was straight, her expression neutral.

Just another invisible member of the kitchen staff.

Charlotte sat in her classroom during her free period, laptop open, watching the video feed from the server room. Angus stood beside her, also focused on the screen.

They'd watched Evans work for the last twenty minutes, typing on his laptop, checking the server, occasionally muttering to himself.

Kaylee appeared in the doorway with a tray. Charlotte leaned closer to the screen. "Here we go."

They watched Kaylee enter, set down the tray, and offer Evans tea. She was calm, professional, natural, with no sign of nervousness.

Then she moved closer to Evans, crouched down and retied her shoelace.

"She's going to try now," Angus murmured.

Charlotte held her breath.

Kaylee's hand moved so quickly that Charlotte almost missed it. One moment her hand was in her pocket, then it was touching the laptop bag, then she was standing up.

Angus frowned. "Did she—?"

Kaylee said something to Evans, then left.

Charlotte immediately opened another window on her laptop: the audio feed from the bug.

Static. Then the sound of typing and Evans's voice muttering "Come on, decrypt already…"

Charlotte grinned. "She did it. The bug's active."

Angus let out a breath. "She's good."

"She really is."

They watched Evans work on the server. Now they could see him on camera and hear everything he said. Complete surveillance.

Charlotte pulled out her phone and texted Kaylee: *Well done.*

A minute later, Kaylee replied: *Glad it worked. Nearly had a heart attack when he called me back at the end.*

Charlotte smiled: *You did brilliantly. Thank you.*

On-screen, Evans was still working away, oblivious to the fact that every word he said and every move he made was being recorded.

Charlotte settled back in her chair. "Now we wait and see what he does. Who he calls, where he goes."

"And if he contacts the boys?"

"We'll have it on tape."

Angus glanced at his watch. "Your next lesson's in ten minutes."

"I know. I'll keep the audio feed running on my phone. If anything important happens, I'll hear it."

She saved the video footage, marked the timestamp where Kaylee had planted the bug, and backed everything up. Then she closed the laptop and stood up. "Right, time for year 8 computing. More binary conversions."

"Thrilling."

"Hey, binary's important. It's literally how computers work."

Angus smiled. "You're really getting into this teaching thing, aren't you?"

Charlotte paused. "You know what? I am. When we're not investigating criminal operations, I might do some more. It's quite satisfying."

"Maybe you've found your calling."

She shook her head. "I like it, but not enough to change careers. And I suspect Freddie won't want me back when all this comes out."

Angus grinned. "Probably not."

Angus was halfway through his lunch when a year 8 boy appeared at the refectory door, red-faced and out of breath.

"Sir! Mr Harper! There's a boy locked in the changing rooms and he won't come out."

Angus put down his fork. "Which boy?"

"Josh King, sir. He's in one of the toilet cubicles. He's been in there since the end of PE and he won't open the door."

"How long ago was that?"

"Twenty minutes, sir. Maybe more."

Angus stood up. Sophie's voice was immediately in his head: never go into the changing rooms alone. He scanned the staff table. Sandbrook was deep in conversation with Sarah Hartley. Neither of them had noticed. The rest of the teachers were either eating or on their phones.

"Mr Sandbrook," Angus said. "Could I borrow you for a minute?"

Sandbrook glanced up, a forkful of pasta halfway to his mouth. "Now?"

"Yes. Now."

Sandbrook sighed, put down his fork, and followed Angus out of the refectory. The year 8 boy trotted alongside them.

"What's happened?" Sandbrook asked.

"A boy's locked himself in the changing room toilets."

"Who is it?"

"Josh King, Year 8."

Sandbrook groaned.

They reached the changing rooms. Angus pushed open the main door and the smell hit him: damp towels, sweat, and deodorant.

The room was empty.

At the far end, one of the cubicle doors was shut. Angus could see a pair of trainers underneath it.

He turned to the year 8 boy. "Right, off you go. Back to the refectory."

"But sir—"

"Go."

The boy left reluctantly. Angus and Sandbrook walked to the cubicle.

"Josh?" Angus said. "It's Mr Harper. Mr Sandbrook is here too. Are you all right?"

Silence.

"Josh, I need you to talk to me. No one's in trouble."

"I'm not coming out."

"Okay. Can you tell me why?"

Silence again, then, "Someone's taken my trousers."

Angus closed his eyes briefly. He'd talked a man off a bridge, he'd kept a woman on the phone for an hour while armed response moved into position outside a flat in Newton Abbot, and now he was negotiating with a teenager over a pair of missing trousers.

"Your school trousers?"

"Yes. And my pants. They've taken everything. I've only got my PE kit on, and I can't go to afternoon lessons in PE kit. I'll get a detention."

"You won't get a detention. I'll make sure of that. Do you know who took them?"

"No." The voice wobbled. "They were on the bench, and when I came out of the shower they were gone. All of them. My shirt's gone too."

Sandbrook mouthed "bullying" at Angus and rolled his eyes, which Angus did not appreciate. This was clearly not funny to the boy behind the door.

"Josh, listen to me. We're going to sort this out. I'm going to find your clothes, and if I can't find them, I'll get you a spare set from somewhere. But I need you to come out of the cubicle."

"No."

"Why not?"

"Because if I come out, everyone will know I was hiding in here and they'll call me a baby."

Angus recognised the logic. It was the same logic he'd heard from suspects who'd barricaded themselves in bedrooms and attics. The longer you stayed, the harder it was to come out, because coming out meant facing whatever was on the other side. The situation fed on itself.

"Josh, there's no one here except me and Mr Sandbrook.

Everyone else is at lunch. If you come out now, no one will see you. But the longer you stay in there, the more people will notice you're missing, and then it becomes a bigger deal than it needs to be."

He kept his voice calm, steady, exactly the way he'd been trained. Low pitch. No urgency. Give them time to process.

Sandbrook shifted impatiently. Angus held up a hand: wait.

Thirty seconds passed. Then the bolt slid back, and the door opened slowly. Josh stood there in his PE shorts and a vest, eyes red, arms folded tightly across his chest.

"Right," Angus said, keeping his tone matter-of-fact. "Let's find your clothes."

It took less than a minute. Sandbrook found the trousers and shirt behind a radiator at the far end of the changing room. The pants and socks were wedged on top of a high window frame, out of reach unless you stood on a bench.

"Deliberate," Angus murmured to Sandbrook, while Josh got dressed in the cubicle. "Spread across the room so he couldn't find everything at once. That's not a prank, that's systematic."

Sandbrook nodded. "I'll report it to the headmaster."

Josh emerged, fully dressed, tie crooked. He wouldn't make eye contact.

"Josh," Angus said. "Has this happened before?"

The boy shrugged, which meant yes.

"If it happens again, you come and find me. Don't lock yourself away. Come to me, or Mrs Harper, or Matron. Understood?"

Josh nodded.

"Good lad. Now go and get some lunch before they clear the plates."

Josh left without a word. Angus watched him go, then turned to Sandbrook.

"Does this happen a lot?"

Sandbrook shrugged. "More than you'd think. Boys hide each other's clothes, chuck shoes on the roof, that sort of thing. It's just what they do. He'll be fine. They always are." Sandbrook headed for the door.

Angus stood alone in the changing room for a moment. He wasn't so sure about that.

CHAPTER 32

Charlotte sat in her classroom after school had finished, laptop open, earpiece in. The audio feed from Evans's bug had been quiet for the last hour. There was just the sound of him driving, occasional traffic noise, classical music from the radio.

She was staring out of the window, half listening, when Evans's voice came through clearly. He'd fixed the virus, although it had taken him a few hours. *Not bad at all,* Charlotte thought.

"Right, let's see what we've got."

The car noise stopped and a door closed with a thunk. He must have arrived at his office.

Charlotte focused on the audio. Footsteps. A chair scraping. The familiar startup music of a computer.

"Come on, load already, you stupid f***ing piece of s**t," Evans muttered.

Charlotte tutted.

The keyboard clicked, then silence. Charlotte could hear him breathing.

"What the..."

More keyboard clicks, rapid now, then the sound of audio

rewinding, followed by the tinny sound of video playback through laptop speakers.

"Who's that?" Evans said, his voice tight.

Charlotte's stomach clenched. Video? From where?

Then she heard him rummaging for something and the familiar sound of a phone ringing.

"We have a problem," he said, without preamble. "The new computing teacher. I've got her on video in the server room at five in the morning."

Oh God. Charlotte's mind raced. The server room that morning, when she'd planted the video camera. Evans had seen her. But how?

She couldn't hear the reply. Who was he speaking to?

"So, this Bridget Harper," he said. "What do you know about her?"

Silence as the other person spoke and he listened.

"I'm telling you I can see her, plain as day, doing something in the server room at stupid o'clock. I can't see what she's doing, but she doesn't touch the server. I'm googling her now. Do you think she planted the virus?"

More silence.

"Well, keep an eye on her and I'll probe a bit more. See what I can find out about her. I'm on the school server now."

Charlotte swallowed. He would be checking out the fake identity Freddie had created for her.

"This says she's a career changer, a former local government officer with a computing degree from Bristol. No, that doesn't add up."

Charlotte put her head in her hands.

"Previous employment, St Mary's School in the Cayman Islands." A snort. "Very convenient." Then a pause. "I need you to go to the server room and take a look. See if you can spot what she did. I'll send the video over so you can see."

So whoever he was speaking to was in the school.

Evans was quiet for a moment. "She definitely didn't

touch the server. Luckily, it was unaffected by the virus. Everything's still running just fine."

Charlotte pulled out her phone and texted Angus: *Evans saw me in the server room this morning – he must have his own camera. Call me NOW.*

"Find out all you can about Bridget Harper," Evans said. "After you've checked the server room. Call back if you find something."

The call ended. Evans exhaled heavily. Charlotte heard him moving around, the sound of drawers opening. He was packing something.

Silence. Then the sound of his laptop closing, footsteps, a door opening and closing.

Charlotte pulled out her earpiece. "Shit," she muttered. He'd admitted he was using the server, though. That was big.

She turned to her laptop. She needed the server decrypted to see what was going on. And who had he been speaking to?"

Her phone buzzed. Angus, calling her back. He sounded out of breath, and there was a distant sound of boys shouting. Then she remembered he was running the after-school rugby club.

"He knows," she said.

"I'm sorry, what? Who?"

"Evans has security footage of me in the server room early this morning. He's seen it, and now he knows I'm up to something."

Angus was quiet for a moment. "How do you know?"

"The audio bug. I just listened to him reviewing the footage and making a phone call.'"

"Who to? Could you hear who was on the other end of the phone?"

"No. And he didn't mention a name, but it's definitely someone here."

"Did he mention the audio bug?"

"No."

"So we still have an advantage. He thinks he's caught you out, but he doesn't know we can listen in on his little chats."

"What do we do? What happens if Evans's contact finds the camera in the server room? He could go straight to Freddie, or spread it all round school."

Charlotte sighed. "I should have realised this might happen. Of course, Evans would have a contact in school."

"Neither of us did." Angus sounded weary. "Anyway, keep watch on the server-room camera."

"What about Freddie? Do we tell him?"

Angus hesitated. "Not yet. If we tell him now, he'll want to go to the police. We still don't know who the accomplice is. Once we find out, that'll be very useful."

"All right. But Angus... be careful. Evans might try something."

Charlotte ended the call and sat in her classroom, staring at the laptop. She wanted to go to the server room, too, but it would be better to watch remotely.

She pulled up the recording of Evans's phone call and listened to it again, trying to hear the person he was on the phone with. She could make out nothing.

CHAPTER 33

Angus cut through to the science corridor to reach the server room more quickly. It was half past five. Most after-school clubs had finished, and students were dispersing for prep time or activities, so the corridor was quiet.

He slowed as he approached the far end. At the server-room door was a figure. Year 11. Slim build, dark hair.

Harrison.

The boy unlocked the door and slipped inside, pulling the door closed behind him.

Angus stopped at the corner, then ducked into an empty classroom. He pulled out his phone and texted Charlotte: *Harrison's inside. I'm waiting.*

Her reply came quickly: *Watching on video feed. He's at the server rack now.*

Angus leaned against the wall, listening.

Five minutes passed.

The door opened and Harrison emerged, pulling the door shut behind him. His face was pale and drawn.

Angus stepped out. "Harrison."

The boy froze, staring at him.

"What were you doing in there?" Angus asked quietly.

Harrison's mouth opened, then closed again. "I, um... Nothing. I was just—"

"You're working for Evans, aren't you?"

Harrison took a step back. "No. I don't—"

"Don't lie to me." Angus moved closer. "I know about Evans. I know what he's been making you do."

Harrison's face crumpled and he looked everywhere but at Angus. For a moment, Angus thought he might burst into tears or make a run for it. Then the boy's shoulders sagged, all the fight going out of him.

"I can't talk about it," Harrison whispered. "If I do, I'm dead."

"If you don't, more people will get hurt." Angus kept his voice gentle but firm. "Oliver tried to get out, didn't he?"

Harrison flinched at Oliver's name.

They turned at the sound of footsteps behind them. Charlotte was there, slightly out of breath. She must have run from her classroom.

"Harrison," she said, "we know someone is pressuring you into working for them."

Harrison stared at her. "What? How?"

"We've been investigating," Charlotte said. "We know you're a victim. You've been blackmailed. But we need you to tell us everything."

Harrison shook his head. "I can't. Evans has evidence of what I've done. If I say anything, he'll—"

"He'll what?" Angus asked. "Send you to prison? Harrison, you're seventeen. Evans is an adult who manipulated you into committing crimes. That's exploitation. The courts will see that."

"My parents," Harrison said, his voice breaking. "They'll find out. My university applications. Everything I've worked for..."

"Everything you've worked for is already at risk," Charlotte said. "Because Evans won't stop. He'll keep using you until you break or you get caught. Just like Oliver."

Harrison's hands were shaking. He looked between them, trapped.

"We're going to the headmaster," Angus said. "You're coming with us."

"No. Please—"

"You don't have a choice," Charlotte said. "This ends today. One way or another."

Harrison closed his eyes. But he didn't resist as Angus gently took his arm and guided him down the corridor.

Freddie's office was warm, the late-afternoon sun streaming through the windows. The headmaster sat behind his desk, his face grave. Charlotte and Angus sat, facing him. Harrison slumped in a third chair, hunched over, staring at his hands.

"Right," Freddie said. "Someone needs to explain what's going on."

Angus glanced at Charlotte, then spoke. "Harrison's been working on the school servers after hours. We have video evidence of him entering the server room just now."

Freddie looked at Harrison. "Is this true?"

Harrison didn't respond.

"Harrison," Freddie said, his voice firm but not unkind. "Look at me."

The boy slowly raised his head.

"What were you doing in the server room?"

The boy stayed silent.

"We know you've been accessing the servers," Charlotte said. "We have timestamps, login records, everything. We just need you to tell us why."

Harrison shook his head.

Freddie leaned forward. "Harrison, I've known you since

you were in Year 7. You're a good student. You work hard. Whatever's happened, whatever you've done, we can work through it. But you need to talk to us."

"I can't," Harrison whispered.

"Why not?"

"Because…" Harrison swallowed. "Because if I do, my life is over."

"Your life isn't over, Harrison," Angus said. "But it will be if you keep protecting the person who's been using you."

Harrison looked up sharply. "You don't understand. He has proof. He has everything. If I talk—" He stopped, realising he'd said too much.

"Who has proof?" Freddie asked. "Who's 'he'?"

Harrison didn't respond, but tears ran down his cheeks.

"Harrison, we know about Evans," said Charlotte. "We know he's been running something dodgy, using the school network. He's been pressuring you, hasn't he? Oliver, you, and some others. I need you to tell me the key to decrypt the server."

Harrison looked up, his eyes wide. "I can't."

Freddie stood up and walked around his desk, sitting on the edge so that he was closer to Harrison's level. "Harrison, listen to me. Whatever Mr Evans has on you, whatever evidence he claims to have, it doesn't matter. What he's done to you is a crime. He's an adult in a position of trust, who has exploited a minor. That's illegal. The police will see that. No one blames you."

"The police?" Harrison's voice shot up in panic. "You're going to call the police?"

"We have to," Freddie said gently. "If what Mrs Harper and Mr Harper are saying is true, a serious crime has been committed. Multiple crimes. We can't just ignore that."

Harrison stood up abruptly. "No. No, you can't. Please. I haven't done anything wrong. I was just— I was checking the computers. That's all. Just routine maintenance."

"At half past four on a Tuesday?" Charlotte asked. "Without authorisation?"

"I had permission. From Mr Evans. He asked me to check something."

"What did he ask you to check?" Angus asked.

Harrison shrugged. "Network connectivity. Making sure everything was running properly after the virus this morning."

"Why would Mr Evans ask you to do that?" Freddie asked. "You're a student, not an IT technician, and he was here earlier today."

"I'm good with computers. He knows that. He sometimes asks me to help with small things."

Charlotte leaned forward. "Harrison, I checked the server logs. We know you weren't just checking connectivity. You were accessing specific files and transferring data. What were you doing?"

"Nothing. I wasn't doing anything."

"I don't believe you," said Angus.

"I was just looking around. Making sure everything was okay."

Freddie rubbed his face. "Harrison, this isn't helping. If you won't talk to us, I'll have to call your parents. And I'll also have to call the police. They'll want to examine the servers and check what you were doing."

Harrison stood frozen to the spot. His breathing was getting faster and more shallow. "I can't tell you. I'm sorry, I just can't."

"Why not?" Charlotte asked, her voice softer now. "What is Mr Evans threatening you with?"

Harrison's eyes filled with tears. "Everything. He's threatening me with everything. If I talk, he shows the evidence to the police, my parents, the universities I've applied to. He destroys my life, that's what he does. That's what he did to Oliver."

"Oliver tried to tell someone," Angus said quietly. "Is that what happened?"

Harrison nodded, tears spilling over. "He tried to tell his parents. And Evans made sure Oliver's life fell apart. He made it look like Oliver was unstable. Disturbed. And then Oliver couldn't take it any more..." Harrison couldn't finish.

The room was silent.

Freddie's face had gone very pale. "Evans did that? To Oliver?"

Harrison nodded. "And he'll do it to me, too, if I talk. He'll make sure everyone knows what I did. He has screenshots, timestamps, messages. Everything. I'll go to prison."

"You won't go to prison," Charlotte said firmly. "You're a victim."

"You don't know that," Harrison said, his voice rising. "You can't promise that. And even if I don't go to prison, my parents will know. Cambridge will know. Everyone will know I'm a criminal."

"Or," Angus said, "everyone will know you're the brave person who helped stop a predator from hurting more kids."

Harrison stared at him.

"You can be the victim who stays silent," Angus continued, "or you can be the hero who speaks up. It's your choice."

Harrison sank back into his chair, put his head in his hands and sobbed.

Freddie looked at Charlotte and Angus, his expression asking, *What do we do?*

They sat in silence, letting Harrison cry.

Finally, after what felt like an eternity, Harrison looked up. His face was blotchy, his eyes swollen. "If I tell you," he said, his voice hoarse, "can you promise I'll be protected? From Evans?"

"Yes," Freddie said immediately. "We'll make sure you're safe."

"And my parents? Do they have to know?"

Freddie hesitated. "I can't promise about that. But I can promise that we'll do everything we can to minimise the damage. For you, and for the other boys involved."

Harrison took a shaky breath. "There are others: Thomas and Christopher. They're still working for him too."

"We need to hear it from you," said Freddie. "How it started. What Evans made you do. How he controlled you."

Harrison closed his eyes. When he opened them again, there was resignation in his face. "All right, I'll tell you. But you have to promise to protect Thomas and Christopher too. They're just as scared as I am."

"We will," Freddie said. "You have my word."

CHAPTER 34

Harrison's hands were still shaking as he typed his password into the server login screen. They were using Freddie's computer to connect because Evans still had a camera somewhere in the server room.

"Take your time," Charlotte said quietly.

Harrison's fingers hovered over the keyboard. "If Evans checks the logs, he'll see I accessed this. He'll know I talked."

"We're past that now," Freddie said. "You're protected. Whatever happens next, we'll make sure you're safe."

Harrison took a deep breath, then nodded and continued typing. A command prompt appeared.

"The encrypted folder is here," Harrison said, navigating through directories. "But you need the decryption key to access the files."

"Can you provide it?" Charlotte asked.

Harrison hesitated. "If I give you the key, there's no going back. Evans will know someone's accessed the files. He has alerts set up."

"He already knows someone's on his trail," Angus said. "He saw Mrs Harper on his security camera this morning. That's why we need to move fast."

"The key, Harrison," said Charlotte. "Please."

Harrison closed his eyes for a moment, then typed a long string of characters and hit enter.

For a moment, nothing happened. Then the folder unlocked, revealing hundreds of files. He stood up, and Charlotte took his place in the chair.

Charlotte opened the first spreadsheet and her stomach dropped. "Jesus," she whispered.

Angus leaned over. "What is it?"

Charlotte scrolled through the data. Row after row after row. Not hundreds of entries – thousands. Tens of thousands.

"So much data," she said quietly.

She opened another file, then another. The scope was staggering.

ST ATHELSTAN'S SCHOOL - 312 student records
HARROW PREPARATORY - 445 student records
WESTMINSTER COLLEGE - 521 student records
ETON PREPARATORY - 389 student records
CHELTENHAM LADIES' - 402 student records

"Five schools," Freddie said, his voice hollow. "He had contracts with five private schools."

"Not just five schools," Charlotte said, scrolling further. "Look."

More folders appeared:

NHS_PATIENT_DATA - 1,434,782 records
HMRC_TAX_RECORDS - 4,809,934 records
UK_PASSPORT_OFFICE - 604,421 records
DVLA_LICENCE_DATA - 124,338 records
CREDIT_REFERENCE_AGENCIES - 2,330,557 records

• • •

"I wasn't expecting this," Angus said.

Charlotte opened the NHS folder. Medical records with complete patient histories. Diagnoses, medications, mental health records. Everything.

"He wasn't just stealing school data," she said. "He had access to government databases. NHS systems. Tax records. Passports. Drivers' licences. Credit histories."

"How?" Freddie asked, staring at the screen. "How is that even possible?"

"His IT company," Charlotte replied. "He had contracts with schools, but he also had government contracts. He maintained the IT systems of NHS trusts, local councils, and HMRC regional offices. Which meant that he had admin access to their networks."

She pulled up another spreadsheet: transaction logs. Each entry showed what data had been sold, and for how much.

NHS patient record bundle (500 records) – SOLD to Client_RU_447 for £45,000

HMRC tax records (200 high-net-worth individuals) – SOLD to Client_CN_893 for £68,000

Passport data (1000 records) – SOLD to Client_RU_621 for £125,000

Credit histories (500 records) – SOLD to Client_EE_244 for £32,000

The list was staggering.

"RU, CN, EE," Angus said, reading the client codes. "Russia, China, Eastern Europe?"

"Yes," Harrison said. "Evans sold data to organised crime

groups. Identity-theft rings, scammers – anyone who would pay."

Charlotte scrolled through the transaction history. "He's made nearly five million pounds." She turned to Freddie. "This isn't a small operation: it's industrial-scale data theft. Evans has been harvesting and selling sensitive personal data from government systems for years."

"If he's supplying criminals worldwide," Angus said, "this data has probably been used to steal millions from innocent people."

Freddie had turned even paler. "You're telling me that a man hired to manage our IT systems has been stealing government data and selling it to criminals? For years?"

"Harrison," Charlotte said gently. "What exactly did Evans have you doing?"

"At first, just keeping an eye on the server. Then he started asking me to help with other things. With accessing NHS patient records and tax information. He said it was to identify security vulnerabilities so they could be fixed. And he was paying us all."

"I see," Angus said.

"I knew he was stealing the data. Packaging and selling it." Harrison looked at his hands. "I helped him steal information from thousands of people. I knew it was wrong, but by the time I realised what was really happening, he had evidence of everything I'd done. He said that if I stopped, he'd make sure I went to prison for decades."

"Oliver wanted out, didn't he?" Charlotte asked.

Harrison nodded. "Oliver discovered that his own father's tax records had been stolen and sold. His mother's medical history. Their passport numbers. All of it ended up on the dark web. He was furious."

"And he knew he'd helped to make it happen."

"He tried to tell Evans he wanted out and Evans threatened him. A teacher in the school is helping Evans. I don't know who it is, but Evans says they'll hurt us if we say anything. With Oliver, it wasn't a suicide attempt, but it was made to look like one."

Angus shook his head. "No wonder you were scared."

"This isn't just about the school," Charlotte said. "This is a major cybercrime operation. We need the National Crime Agency and the Cyber Crime Unit. This is way beyond local police."

Freddie pulled out his phone. "I'll call them now."

"Wait," Angus said. "If we call them now, Evans will see the activity on his network and know he's been compromised. He could wipe the servers, destroy the evidence, and run."

"So what *do* we do?" Freddie asked.

Charlotte thought for a moment. "We set a trap and find out who's helping Evans at the school. We won't call local police. We'll contact the NCA directly and have them coordinate with Cyber Crimes. They'll know how to preserve digital evidence and stop Evans from destroying data."

She looked at Harrison. "But we have to move fast. If Evans checks his security footage again, or if he realises we've accessed these files, people could get hurt. Not just us. The other boys too. Anyone he thinks is a threat."

Harrison sat up slightly. "Then let's do it. Let's stop him before he hurts anyone else."

Charlotte took out her phone and rang her brother, DCI Mark Lockwood. He'd put her on a fast track to the right person at the NCA.

CHAPTER 35

Twenty minutes later, Charlotte and Angus crouched in the chapel gallery, high above the side room. They'd placed three cameras in strategic positions and two audio bugs. Charlotte's laptop showed feeds from all angles.

Harrison was safely back in his dormitory. He'd texted Evans from Freddie's office, then been escorted away before Evans could arrive.

Charlotte's phone buzzed. A text from Kaylee: *In position. Ready.*

Now Kaylee was in the small vestry at the back of the chapel, the only other exit from the side room. If Evans tried to run, Kaylee would see him.

Charlotte texted back: *Stay hidden. Don't engage unless absolutely necessary.*

I know. I'll be careful.

The main chapel door opened. Evans entered, looking around warily. "Harrison?" he called. When there was no reply, he cursed, then muttered, "Stupid boy."

"Jeremy, what are you doing in school?" said a voice from the doorway. It was Mrs Hodge, the matron.

Charlotte looked at Angus and rolled her eyes. The last thing they needed was Matron disturbing their trap.

Evans turned. "Have you seen Harrison?" he asked. "He called me with some garbled message about the server and the new computing teacher, Mrs Harper."

She frowned. "What? No, I've not seen him. Is the server all right? What's he been doing to it? Is the data safe?"

Charlotte and Angus shared a glance. So Mrs Hodge was Evans's accomplice in the school.

Freddie stepped out of the shadows near the altar. "Mrs Hodge, you're the person who's been helping Evans?"

Charlotte and Angus stood up too: there was no point in hiding. The three people below couldn't see them, though.

Harrison is safe," Freddie continued. "And well out of reach of you two."

"Headmaster," said Mrs Hodge, her voice controlled, "what's going on? Jeremy said Harrison called him, talking about some kind of emergency."

"There is an emergency," Freddie said coldly. "Just not the kind you were expecting. It's over. We know about the data server and how you've been manipulating boys into helping you."

Evans eyed the exit. "I don't think—"

"The police will be here any minute," Freddie said.

"I must say, Headmaster, this is highly irregular," said Mrs Hodge. "What's going on? If you have concerns about Harrison Cole, you should have spoken to me directly. I'm responsible for student welfare."

"Are you?" Freddie asked. "Because from what I've learned today, I believe you've been doing the exact opposite of ensuring student welfare."

Mrs Hodge blinked. "I don't know what you mean."

"Yes, you do." Freddie moved towards her. "I know about the data-theft operation. I know about the students you recruited. I know about Oliver Sutherland."

Evans's eyes darted around the chapel, looking for an escape.

Angus nudged Charlotte and indicated the gallery steps leading down to the chapel. Quietly, they descended.

Mrs Hodge managed a tight smile. "That's a very serious accusation you're making, Headmaster. What evidence do you have?"

"Server logs. Transaction records. Over four million pounds in stolen data sales. NHS records, tax information, passport data." Freddie raised his eyebrows. "Shall I continue?"

Evans took a step backwards. "I don't have to listen to this rubbish. I'm leaving."

"No, you're not." Freddie didn't raise his voice. "You've both used and abused this school and its pupils. If you think I'm going to let you walk out of here, you've got another think coming."

Mrs Hodge looked at Evans, her eyes narrowed. "You idiot. I told you to be more careful," she muttered. "You should have shut Harrison up."

"Harrison's a victim," Freddie said. "As are Thomas and Christopher. As was Oliver."

"Oliver's unstable," said Mrs Hodge. "I documented his deteriorating mental health. Paranoid, delusional—"

"He was being blackmailed," Freddie cut in. "By both of you. You recruited him, used him to steal data, and when he tried to escape your clutches, you destroyed his credibility so that no one would believe him. Then when he tried to escape from it, you attacked him and made it look like a suicide."

Mrs Hodge drew herself up. "My record at this school is impeccable. I've given twenty years of dedicated service. The governors trust me; the parents trust me. It's your word against mine, Headmaster, and we both know who they'll believe."

"Perhaps," Freddie said. "But it's not just my word."

He gestured towards the ceiling. "Everything you've said in this room has been recorded. Every single word."

Mrs Hodge's eyes widened, then narrowed. She looked around the room, searching for the cameras.

Evans's face had gone white. "You recorded us? Without consent? That's—"

"Legal, when investigating a serious crime." Angus stepped forward. "Which this certainly is."

Mrs Hodge turned to the door. "I'm leaving. This is harassment, at the very least."

When she opened it, Kaylee was standing in the vestry, phone held up and recording.

"I wouldn't try it," Kaylee said quietly.

Mrs Hodge stared at her. "You. Kitchen staff. Get out of my way."

"No."

Mrs Hodge's face flushed with anger. "Move. *Now*."

"I said no." Kaylee didn't move an inch. "I'm recording too. I've got everything you just said. About Oliver, the other boys, and your 'impeccable record.'"

"You little—" Mrs Hodge lunged forward, hands reaching for Kaylee's phone.

Kaylee stepped back, keeping the phone out of reach. "If you touch me, that's assault. On camera."

Mrs Hodge ran at her.

Kaylee twisted sideways, letting Mrs Hodge's momentum carry her forward. Then she stuck out her foot and Mrs Hodge stumbled into a stack of hymn books. She went down hard, tangled in the strap of her own handbag.

"Kaylee!" Charlotte was already running to her. "Are you all right?"

But Kaylee stood her ground, her phone still pointing at Mrs Hodge, who was struggling to get up.

"Stay down," Kaylee said, her voice shaking but firm. "You're going nowhere."

Evans was frozen in the doorway. He looked at Mrs Hodge on the floor, at Kaylee blocking the exit, at Freddie behind him, and his shoulders sagged.

"Yes," Freddie said. "It's over."

Charlotte reached them. "Kaylee, are you okay?"

"I'm fine." Kaylee was breathing hard and her hands shook. But she kept the phone steady, still recording.

Mrs Hodge finally got to her feet, her face twisted with fury. "You have no idea what you've done. That recording is inadmissible in any court of law. I'll sue you for assault."

"You assaulted her," Angus pointed out. "We all saw it. Multiple cameras caught it."

Mrs Hodge huffed and stormed off.

"That was incredibly stupid," Charlotte told Kaylee.

Kaylee's face fell. "I thought—"

"And incredibly brave," Charlotte continued, a smile breaking through. "You stopped her from running. You kept recording. You didn't back down when she threatened you."

"Perfect self-defence," Angus said. "You did everything exactly right."

Kaylee looked down at her phone, still clutched in her hand. "I got it all. Everything she said about Oliver, about the other boys, about her record. It's all here."

They stood in the chapel for a moment, the weight of everything settling over them.

"Now we just need the police," said Charlotte. "Any idea of their ETA?"

"Hopefully, any minute," said Freddie.

"We need to keep Evans away from the server room," Charlotte said. "We can't let him destroy evidence."

"I'm on it," Freddie said, positioning himself between Evans and the exit.

Evans slumped into a nearby pew and put his head in his hands.

Mrs Hodge stood rigid, her face a mask of fury. "This is harassment. I'll have you all brought before the governors—"

"Save it for your solicitor," Angus said calmly.

CHAPTER 36

Two weeks later, Freddie drove to Angus's house to update them in person.

Angus answered the door, smiling. "Freddie! Come in, it's good to see you. Tea?"

"Please." He followed Angus through to the living room, where Kaylee was relaxing on the sofa next to Charlotte.

"Hello, Headmaster," Kaylee said, with a smile.

"Kaylee, you're looking well. You, too, Charlotte. How are you both?"

They settled in the living room with mugs of tea.

"So, you wanted an update. Evans and Hodge have both been charged with multiple crimes under the Computer Misuse Act and the Data Protection Act, as well as fraud, conspiracy, and child exploitation. The CPS think they have an airtight case, although investigations are ongoing."

"That's good," Charlotte said.

"Evans is cooperating fully, trying for a reduced sentence. He's given up his buyers, his methods, everything."

"And Hodge?" Angus asked.

"Refusing to cooperate. She hired an expensive solicitor and she's maintaining she did nothing wrong." Freddie's expression hardened. "But the evidence against her is overwhelming. The profiles she kept of vulnerable students, her communications with Evans, the testimony from the boys. She'll go to prison."

"Good," Kaylee said quietly.

"Mark Harrison, Thomas, and Christopher are all receiving counselling. They're victims, not criminals." Freddie's expression softened. "Harrison's doing better. His parents have been incredibly supportive. Oh, and he admitted stealing your laptop, Charlotte, but he was told to do it."

"And Oliver?" Charlotte asked.

"He's out of hospital. Living at home, taking things slowly. But he's improving. He's even talking about finishing his A-levels." Freddie smiled. "His parents want to thank you, by the way. All of you."

"We just did our job," Charlotte said. "Although, it's always good to stop criminal activity like this. Shocking doesn't even begin to describe it. How are things at the school, generally?"

Freddie set down his mug. "We're getting back to normal. The scandal hit the press, as expected. You probably saw it? The governors were furious. Some parents withdrew their children. But we're weathering it."

"You'll survive," Angus said. "You took action when you discovered the problem. That counts for something."

"I hope so." Freddie turned to Kaylee. "Which brings me to you. I wanted to offer you your job back. Properly this time. A permanent contract, better wages, proper accommodation in the staff quarters. You proved yourself a good worker, and what's more, essential to the investigation. The school would be lucky to have you."

Kaylee opened her mouth to respond, but Angus interrupted.

"Actually, Freddie, Charlotte and I have been talking." He turned to Kaylee. "If you'd be interested, Kaylee, we could use an extra pair of hands with our cases. What do you think?"

Kaylee's eyes widened. "You want me to work with you?"

"You're observant, resourceful, and brave," Charlotte said. "You planted that bug on Evans without him noticing. You stood up to Hodge when she tried to run. You kept your head in a genuinely dangerous situation."

"We'd train you properly, of course," Angus added. "Investigation techniques, surveillance, technical skills. But the instincts? You already have those."

Kaylee looked between them, stunned. Then she smiled slowly. "Depends on the pay."

Angus laughed. "I'm sure we can come to a very amicable arrangement."

"Better than kitchen wages, anyway," Charlotte said. "Or supermarket pay."

Kaylee grinned. "I accept."

Freddie picked up his mug and drained it. "Congratulations. Though I have to admit, I'm disappointed. You would have made an excellent addition to our staff."

"Thanks," Kaylee said.

After Freddie had left, the three of them sat in the living room.

"So," Kaylee said, eventually. "I'm a private investigator now?"

"Junior investigator," Charlotte corrected, gently. "You'll be learning as you go."

"Still beats peeling potatoes," Kaylee said.

"True," Angus agreed. "Though the potatoes don't usually try to assault you."

Charlotte raised her mug. "To new beginnings."

Angus and Kaylee raised theirs. "To new beginnings," they echoed.

"Right," Charlotte said, setting down her mug. "If we're

doing this, we start training immediately. First lesson: how to pick a lock."

Kaylee leaned forward eagerly as Charlotte pulled out her lockpick set and a lock from her bag. "I'll order you your own set later."

Angus shook his head. "I thought you'd teach her how to hack a Wi-Fi first."

Charlotte grinned. "That's lesson two, tomorrow."

THE END

I hope you enjoyed this book. If you did, I'd really appreciate it if you could leave a review wherever you bought it. It really helps other people find my books.

You can sign up to my email list to get occasional emails about my latest news and books to your inbox. Go to my website:

www.suzybussell.com

www.ingramcontent.com/pod-product-compliance
Lightning Source LLC
La Vergne TN
LVHW010058110826
845155LV00028B/397

* 9 7 8 1 9 1 5 7 1 7 4 4 3 *